BRIGHT FIGURES SINISTER SHADOWS

SHORT STORIES WITH UNEXPECTED ENDINGS

PAUL D. ELLNER

For Toby,
With best regards,

Paul

4/2/18

ISBN 978-1-63492-662-1

Published by BookLocker.com, Inc., St. Petersburg, Florida.

Printed on acid-free paper.

The characters and events in this book are fictitious. Any similarity to real persons, living or dead, is coincidental and not intended by the author.

BookLocker.com, Inc.
2017

First Edition

For Connie with love

CONTENTS

ABOUT THESE STORIES

My attraction to short stories with surprising conclusions was initiated when I read *The Lady, or the Tiger?* by Frank Stockton. The ending was tantalizing. Short stories have the appeal that one gets to meet the protagonist, learn about his or her particular problem, and enjoy the final resolution all in one sitting. Soon after reading *The Lady, or the Tiger?* I read *An Occurrence at Owl Creek Bridge* by Ambrose Bierce and was stunned by the last line. In time, I found other stories with surprising endings. Some of these were *The Most Dangerous Game* by Richard Connell, *The Devil and Daniel Webster* by Stephen Vincent Benet, and several of the stories in Ray Bradbury's *The Martian Chronicles.* Rod Serling's T.V. series *The Twilight Zone* typified such stories. I liked the "twist" at the end.

I have tried to craft similar stories here. The endings may be startling, amusing, or cause you to ponder for a moment or two. I hope that you may find one or two pleasing.

P.D.E.

STIGMATA

At 5:20 on a spring afternoon, Doctor George Rosen pulled into the parking lot of the Piggly-Wiggly Market in Gainesville, Florida. He jumped out of his car and hurried into the market, pausing only to steal a quick glance at the checkout line. *Yes, Lori was there.* Consulting the list Evelyn had given him, he grabbed a cart and started shopping. He soon finished and took his place in the checkout line.

As the line shortened, George started to unload his cart in preparation for checkout. His heart began to beat faster. He could not keep his eyes off Lori. She was beautiful. When it was his turn, she recognized him with a ready smile.

"Hi, Dr. Rosen."

He had to clear his throat before responding. "Hi, Lori, how are you today?"

"I'm just fine," she said. Then in a lower voice she added, "When will we take those pictures?"

"Soon, Lori. In the next few days, I'll let you know."

"Okay," she smiled. "Bye."

Lori was about 20, with large blue eyes, a pert nose, and a wide mouth. Her dark hair was pulled back into a ponytail secured with a rubber band. Her white blouse, which failed to conceal the cleavage of her young breasts, bore a nametag that read "Lori Sue" and her black pedal pushers were tight enough to accentuate her round bottom and long legs.

George was an instructor in Pharmacology at the University of Florida, his first position since receiving his Ph.D. At 32, he was one of the youngest researchers there. He and Evelyn had purchased a small house not far from the medical school and

Priscilla, their three-year old, had started nursery school. George and Evelyn were soon immersed in the town-gown social life. Most of their friends were other young faculty members. George played poker once a week with some colleagues who referred to themselves as the "Committee for Redistribution of Faculty Salaries."

For the past few weeks, George flirted with Lori each time he went shopping. She stirred his loins like no girl ever had. He and Evelyn were married for five years and up till now he never strayed, but this girl was different. He could not help himself. He wanted her, and he plotted to seduce her.

George formulated a plan. He complimented Lori on her looks and suggested she could be a model. She became excited at the idea.

"That's cool. As a matter of fact, I was a runner-up for the Miss Florida contest last year. I always wanted to be a model," Lori gushed. She went on to tell him that she had been a cheerleader at Gainesville High's football games.

Lori considered George. *He works at the medical school—he is some sort of a doctor—so he must be okay.*

"I can take some pictures of you which could be used for model agencies," George told her.

Lori was enthusiastic. "How much will it cost?" she asked.

"Nothing. I'd be glad to do it."

George had planned to meet her after work, drive to a deserted place he knew out in the Palmettos and convince her to pose nude. Then, he would make love to her. At night, George fantasized a naked Laurie beneath him, gasping with passion, her long legs wrapped around his hips, as he . . .

On the day George had arranged to pick up Lori, he was anxious.

"Are you okay, Dr. Rosen?" Grace, his technician asked. "You're acting kind of jumpy."

George assured her he was fine.

At 5:30 he met Lori at the Piggly-Wiggly and drove out into the country. They walked a short distance into the Palmettos where he knew of a small natural pool surrounded by sand.

"This is a good spot," he said.

He posed Lori in sexy positions with the pool in the background and took a number of photos.

"Now we'll take some as if you're going to go skinny-dipping." He directed her to face the pool and remove her blouse. "Take off your bra too, and hold your blouse over your head as if you were just removing it." Lori complied without hesitation. "That's great," he said, and took a few shots. At this point, George planned to tell her to turn around and face him so that he could feast his eyes on those perky young breasts. Next he would . . .

But then, a stern voice in his head warned. *Whoa boy, do you know what you're doing? You could be in deep shit! Evelyn could find out and divorce you. It would become known. You could lose your job and that would be the end of your career. She's not worth the risk.*

"Okay," he said huskily. "You can get dressed."

Lori seemed disappointed. "Is that all?" She seemed quite willing to share her charms and all the allure of young Southern pulchritude for him and his camera.

During the drive back, Lori seemed confused. "Did you get all the pictures you wanted? Are you sure that's enough?"

"I think they will be fine. I'll have them for you in a few days."

At the market, Lori got out of the car. "Thanks, Dr. Rosen. See you." George could not get away fast enough.

A week later two police officers appeared at George's laboratory. "Are you Dr. George Rosen?" one of them asked.

"Yes, that's me. What can I do for you?"

"Could you please step outside for a minute?" the officer said.

George accompanied them into the hallway. "What's the problem?" he asked.

"We'd like you to come down to the station with us," the officer told him.

"Why? Is this a traffic thing? Has my license expired? What . . ."

"Do you know a Lori Sue Benton?"

"Yes, as a matter of fact, I do. Has anything happened to her?" George's mouth became dry.

"When did you last see her?" the officer asked, ignoring George's question.

"About a week ago, in the market. What are these questions about?"

"She claims that you raped her," the officer said. "Let's go."

George became aware that Grace and some other people stared as he and the police officers walked away.

At the police station he was forced to wait until Lori Sue, accompanied by a police matron, her father and one of the arresting officers, arrived.

"Is this the man you claim to have raped you?" The police officer asked. Lori looked at George, and then turned away.

"Yes, that's him," she whispered.

"Are you certain that he is the man?"

"Yes, I'm sure."

Her father, a burly man, glared at George.

Lori and her father left. The police officer turned to George. "You have the right to remain silent. Anything you say can and will be used against you in a court of law. You have the right to an attorney. If you cannot afford an attorney, one will be provided for you. Do you understand the rights I have just read to you?"

"Yes," George said. He was stunned as he was photographed and fingerprinted.

"You have the right to phone anyone," he told George.

George tried to call Evelyn, but she was not home. He had to wait several hours until he was able to reach her.

"What do you mean you're in jail?" Evelyn asked. "What did you do?"

"Are you alone?" George asked.

"Just me and Prissy."

"I'm accused of raping a girl."

"What?" Evelyn screamed.

"I didn't do it," George said, "but I think I need a lawyer."

George was locked in a cell, where he spent a miserable night.

The next day, a man in a business suit was admitted to George's cell. He handed a business card to George. "I'm Joe Morelli. Your lawyer."

George took a minute to look him over. He was of average height and balding.

"Tell me about it," Morelli said. "Did you do it?"

"No."

"What happened then?" Morelli asked.

"Nothing happened. I just took her out to take some pictures. I didn't touch her."

The lawyer looked unconvinced. "Why were you taking pictures of her?"

"She told me she wanted to be a model. I tried to help her."

"Is that the whole story? You didn't—like hug her or anything?"

George bristled. "I told you I didn't touch her."

"Then why do you think she says you raped her?"

George shook his head. "I don't know."

"Okay, I'm going to try and get you out on bail," Morelli told him as he left.

The following day George stood before a judge with Morelli at his side. An assistant district attorney was present. "You have been charged with rape," the judge said. "How do you plead?"

George looked at Morelli. "Just say 'not guilty.'"

"Not guilty," George told the judge.

Morelli addressed the judge. "Your honor, the defendant is a faculty member at the Medical School and a family man. He's not likely to attempt to flee."

The judge looked at George. "Bail is set at $10,000." The judge looked questioning at the A.D.A., who glanced at George. "That's acceptable to the county," he said. The judge glanced at the docket. "The trial will take place in two weeks."

Morelli drove George home. "Don't leave town," he told George as he dropped him off in front of his house. George could see that some of the neighbors were watching.

George went back to work, but he was aware that his colleagues tried to avoid him. Even Grace was unusually silent. At home, Evelyn said nothing, but she slept in the guest room.

During the next two weeks, George endured the coldness of his colleagues and friends. In the faculty dining room, he was obliged to eat a solo lunch each day.

At 9:00 on a cloudy morning, George entered the courtroom with his lawyer and took his seat at the defense table. He told his lawyer he wanted the opportunity to take the stand and tell his side of the story, but Morelli disagreed. "It'll be better if I do the talking," Morelli told him. George noticed Lori's father and brother. Mr. Benton, a large man, who worked at the feed store in town, looked grim and her brother, a muscular man, glared at George. George thought he saw some of his neighbors and fellow faculty members in the gallery. The assistant district attorney prosecuting the case started by having Lori take the stand, describing Lori as a sweet, innocent, hard-working young woman. Lori testified that George had enticed her into the Palmettos, promising to take some photos, and then attacked her. She went on to describe how she struggled. The prosecutor produced a large photograph of George, naked to the waist. The picture showed four parallel scratch marks running diagonally across George's chest. "I would like to enter this into evidence," he said, and the photo was shown to the jury.

"I don't remember when they took that picture of me," George told Morelli. Morelli stood to cross-examine Lori. After asking her why she had accompanied George into the Palmettos, he asked her why she had not sought medical attention after the alleged incident. Lori blushed and said that she had been too embarrassed. "Ms. Benton, have you ever had Morelli sexual relations before this?" The prosecutor called, "objection, irrelevant," and the judge told Lori to disregard the question.

Morelli sat down, and the prosecutor rested his case.

The jury retired but was back in ten minutes.

"Have you reached a verdict?" the judge asked.

The Foreman nodded and handed the Bailiff a slip of paper.

"The Defendant will rise," the judge ordered. George and Morelli stood. The judge opened the slip of paper. "The jury finds you guilty of rape." George slumped. "I sentence you to be confined in the state penitentiary for three to five years." He banged his gavel.

George rushed over to the bench. "It's not true!" he yelled at the judge. "I'll tell you the truth now. I really wanted to—have sex with her, but I chickened out. I never laid a finger on her."

"Bailiff, remove the Defendant," the judge called. The Bailiff and a deputy rushed forward, pinioned George's arms, handcuffed him and, dragged him from the courtroom.

"I didn't touch her," George screamed. "I didn't touch . . ."

"You didn't touch who?" Evelyn asked. "Wake up, George. You were dreaming."

George opened his eyes. It was dark. He lay in bed with Evelyn next to him. He was covered with sweat.

My God, it was all a dream—just a damn dream.

In the morning George dressed and went down for breakfast. He felt like a new man.

"Good morning, Daddy," Priscilla chirped as he bent to kiss her. Evelyn served him bacon, eggs and grits, poured his coffee and smiled as she sat down at the table.

At work everything was normal. Grace greeted him with a smile and, his friends joined him for lunch.

The prints of the photos he had taken of Lori were delivered to his office. He could not bear to look at them. When he left work, George took the prints and drove to the Piggly-Wiggly. He did not shop but got into Lori's checkout line. When it was his turn, she greeted him with a cheery "Hi, Dr. Rosen. How are you today?"

"Here are the pictures," George said as he handed the photos to her. His hands were shaking. He started to leave.

"Thanks a lot, Dr. Rosen", he heard her call as he left. He would never shop at that market again.

That evening was a quiet one. At bedtime, Evelyn, already in bed, watched George as he pulled on his pajamas.

"George! What happened to your chest?"

George looked down, dismayed to see four parallel scratch marks that ran diagonally across his chest. They had already started to heal.

LANEE'S PEACE

Lanee awoke at dawn and walked to the door of the little hut her husband had built on the roof of their house. She spent the previous night in the hut because the heat in the house was oppressive. She paused for a moment to say her morning prayer to the god of the city and then walked over to look at the field below. The invaders were still there, of course. Their tents spread over the plain as far as the eye could see. They had been there for three weeks waiting for the city to capitulate.

Lanee knew that General Hurtok, their cruel leader, must be among them. For the past three years, Hurtok had ravaged the land, sacking city after city slaughtering the inhabitants.

Lanee was a widow and childless. Two years ago, her husband had collapsed from heat stroke while harvesting grain. The men had carried him back to the house, but he never regained consciousness. Lanee was 30 years old when he died. She studied the tents of the invaders, trying to think of what she could do. Then, an idea came into her head.

Her thoughts were interrupted by the appearance of five city Elders who came to her wearing long faces. In recent years, the Elders had often consulted Lanee because of her wise decisions. "We have come to tell you, Lanee, that our young people want us to surrender. Most of the water in the cisterns is gone. Perhaps if we surrender, they will spare us."

"Listen to me wise Elders, hear my words. We must not surrender! I have a plan, and if our God helps me, we will survive."

"We have listened to your advice before, and it proved to be wise. Tell us of your plan," one of the Elders said.

"I cannot tell you my plan now, but this is what you must do. Tonight after dark, have all of our young men, with their weapons, their swords and spears, silently assemble and hide in the woods on the hill overlooking the enemy camp. Let them wait until dawn when they will hear loud cries from the enemy. Then they must raise a loud shout, charge down at the invaders and slaughter them."

"But Lanee," one of the Elders protested, "the invaders out number us by at least five to one."

"If my plan succeeds," Lanee told them, "the enemy will be confused and running away. Let our army pursue and kill them all."

"We will do as you say, and may our God support you."

Lanee called Nel, her maid, and instructed her to find a large leather bag and fill it with special foods. Then in the afternoon, Lanee bathed in the small amount of water she was allotted, perfumed herself, added color to her lips, and darkened her eyelids. Lanee was a beautiful woman, tall, and slim with long legs. At dusk, accompanied by Nel, she had the men open the city gate to let them leave. The two women walked toward the enemy camp. It was not far since the nearest tents were less than 200 paces from the bottom of the hill on which the city lay.

As they approached the camp, a group of enemy soldiers rushed out, surrounded them, and threatened to kill them. Lanee observed these men were shorter and had darker skin than her people.

"Who are you, and where are you going?" one of them demanded.

"My name is Lanee. I am the Wise Woman of the City." This was a title Lanee had just assumed. "I know our city must fall before your might," she said. "I have come to tell General Hurtok I know of a secret path by which you can take the city without the loss of a single man."

"You have saved your life," one of them said. Her beauty awed the soldiers. "If what you say is true, General Hurtok will indeed be glad to see you."

The soldiers escorted Lanee and Nel to the General's tent. Hurtok came out to see what was happening. The General became quite interested when the soldiers repeated Lanee's message. He looked her over, savoring her beauty like a dog might approach a juicy steak. Hurtok invited her into his tent and sent for his officers. When the officers arrived he turned to Lanee, "Now, lovely lady, tell us of this secret path."

Lanee drew herself up and said, "I am disappointed, General Hurtok. Is this the way you receive one who has come to provide aid?"

Hurtok laughed, and somewhat embarrassed, told his officers, "Of course, she is correct. Come back this evening to my tent, and we will have a banquet. Then, we will learn the secret that will allow us to take the city without the loss of a single man."

The officers departed in high spirits. Hurtok brought Lanee into the rear section of his tent and left her to rest until the banquet. Her maid remained in the front section. A few hours later, the officers returned with food and drink. Lanee was invited to share their food.

"Thank you, gentlemen," she said, "but your food is prohibited to me by our God. Permit me to share our food with you."

She beckoned to her maid who brought the leather bag from which she took out figs, oranges, melons, dates dripping with honey, and fresh baked bread, still warm and fragrant with Zatar. She also produced a large flagon of wine for Hurtok to taste. He was delighted with the foods she brought and after sampling the wine, declared, "This wine is better than ours and far stronger."

They feasted for many hours and drank much wine. Most of them, including Hurtok, were soon drunk. Hurtok staggered to his feet, "I bid you goodnight gentlemen," he said, eyeing Lanee lasciviously.

The officers departed, and Hurtok took Lanee into the rear of his tent where she could see his bed. Hurtok fell onto the bed and watched Lanee as she removed her robe.

"Come," he said to her, holding out his arms. Lanee lay down in his bed, and the General began to make love to her. After a brief encounter, during which Lanee feigned satisfaction, Hurtok fell back and started to fall asleep.

"Is that all?" Lanee asked him. "Surely you have just begun?"

Hurtok rested for a few minutes, then resumed his lovemaking. Once again, Lanee sighed, smiled, and whispered, "That was nice. Let's do it again."

The General struggled, pleaded weariness and told her he needed to sleep. Lanee permitted him 15 minutes and then woke him, expressing desire.

"The men in your city must be stronger and the women more passionate than we imagined," he whispered and attempted another amorous bout. This continued throughout much of the night until finally, after seven episodes, Hurtok fell back completely exhausted. When Lanee was certain he was truly unconscious, she slipped out of bed and put on her robe. The General's sword hung nearby. She picked up the sword. It was heavy. She raised it high over her head and whispered a prayer, then swung it down with all her strength against his neck. It took two more blows before his head rolled off the bed and blood spurted.

She whispered to her maid who slept in the outer section of the tent. "Bring the leather bag," she said. The maid shuddered at the gory sight. Lanee grasped the head by the hair and put it into the bag, and the two women slipped silently out of the tent, past the sleeping sentry, before dawn lighted the sky. They made their way back to the city and called the guard to open the gate. Inside, they sent for the Elders and showed them Hurtok's head.

"Bring a long pole," Lanee directed, "and when daylight comes and you hear a loud commotion and shrieking from the enemy when they discover Hurtock has been killed, put his head on the pole and raise it so the enemy can see it.

Everything went as Lanee predicted. When the pole was raised, there were loud cries from the camp followed by a louder shout as the young army of the city rushed down into the camp killing as many of the enemy as they could, following those who ran away and cutting them down. After the victory, it rained for two weeks, filling the cisterns of the city with water. The invaders who survived left the land and for 20 years there was peace, referred to as the Peace of Lanee.

Lanee never remarried. She became, indeed, the Wise Woman of the City and lived to a ripe old age. The number seven was ever afterwards regarded as a lucky number, although no one knew why.

VORTEX

Even before he opened his eyes, Ed knew he was not where he was supposed to be. The bed was narrow and his exploratory hand failed to find his wife. Opening his eyes, he found he was in a small room. The light came from a round window. It was a porthole. He was in a cabin on a ship.

Edward Parker, forty-one, accountant, lately of Larchmont, New York, had no idea where he was. He remembered locking the door of the house he shared with his wife and two young children, then going to bed. His wife slept, and the two boys were sleeping in the next bedroom. How on earth did I get on this ship, he wondered? Where is it bound?

Ed found his clothes folded on a chair, and he dressed. He opened the door of the cabin and found people rushing through the companionway in panic, paying no attention to him. He followed them and made his way out onto the deck.

The air was chilly under a bright but cloudy sky, and there was a brisk breeze. The sea was calm with a slight swell. People rushed passed him, some walking, others running to lifeboat stations, but Ed could see the davits from which the lifeboats had hung, were now empty. Walking to the rail, he saw a group of lifeboats crowded with women and children, pulling away from the ship. A steward explained to a group of men, "I'm sorry gentlemen, but there are no more boats." Ed became aware the ship was not underway. Her engines were silent, and she listed to one side.

How the hell did I get here, he thought? *Is this a bad dream*? Then, in the distance, he saw the huge floating island of ice, gleaming blue-white, that had mortally wounded the ship.

Soon, the forward section of the ship became much higher, and Ed made his way there. It was like walking up a steep incline.

A dreadful idea formed in his mind. A group of musicians had assembled on the deck, preparing to play. A tall man, with a gray beard, dressed in an officer's uniform stood on the bridge. Ed assumed it was the Captain. The band played a hymn, "Nearer My God to Thee", and the men remaining on deck sang. Some were crying.

Now Ed knew where he was. The angle of the deck became steeper, and the bow pointed to the sky. In the last few seconds, as the huge liner slipped beneath the sea, Ed saw a life preserver hanging on the rail with "RMS Titanic" printed on it. In a moment he was engulfed in the icy water, incredibly cold, struggling to breathe and. . .

Ed became aware of something nibbling on his big toe. He had been dreaming, a nightmare about drowning. Ed explored the nibbling with his other foot, found it was some furry animal, and sat bolt upright. He was in a cell and had been sleeping on a hard pallet of straw. The small animal scurried away. Ed felt dirty and when he passed his hand over his face, he could feel stubble.

Footsteps came down the hall, and a man stopped in front of the cell.

"Where am I, and why am I in a cell?" Ed asked.

The man looked at him curiously. "You're in Cherokee, North Carolina, and we're keepin' you here 'til we hang you in a little bit."

Ed felt his throat get even drier than it had been when he awoke.

"Hang me? What are they hanging me for? I haven't done anything."

The man chuckled. "Not much you haven't," he said, "only stabbed that poor woman to death. We don't cotton to murder and robbery around here, Mr. Dooley."

"Dooley! My name is Edward Parker. You've got the wrong man."

The man laughed again. "I reckon we got the right one. Deputy Grayson tracked you after he found the body. You had the lady's purse and a bloody knife. You was headin' 'cross the mountain to Gatlinburg, over to Tennessee."

Ed's pulse beat faster. "I want a lawyer."

"Too late for that, Tom Dooley. Don't you recollect your trial yesterday?"

Ed grasped the bars with both hands. "No. Is this some kind of a joke?" Ed couldn't remember any trial—his head was muddled, and the only thing he could remember was something about a ship.

"This ain't no joke, Mr. Dooley."

"Tom Dooley is just a song," Ed cried.

"Don't know anything 'bout that, but I don't reckon you'll be singin' much longer. Here comes your party now."

A group of five men came down the corridor and stopped by Ed's cell. They looked grim. One of them wore a star on his vest. He produced a key and opened the cell door. Two of the men walked in, grabbed Ed's arms and tied his hands behind his back. They marched Ed out of the wooden building into the street where a small crowd of men watched.

Ed was hoisted onto a horse. Somebody shoved his feet into the stirrups. The men and the Sheriff mounted their horses. The Sheriff took the bridle of Ed's horse, and the mounted party walked down the dusty street of the small town. Ed's heart pounded in his chest. After ten minutes they came to a meadow where a large tree stood.

"This here white oak will do jes fine," the Sheriff said in a low voice. One of the men threw a rope over a limb and fashioned a noose at the end. The Sheriff backed Ed's horse under the limb and placed the noose over Ed's head and around his neck.

"Please!" Ed cried. "I didn't do it. I'm not the one."

The Sheriff ignored him. "Tom Dooley," he announced in a loud voice, "you have been tried, found guilty, and sentenced to death by hanging."

"No!" Ed screamed. The men backed their horses away. The Sheriff rode up behind Ed's horse and gave it a terrific whack on the flank. The horse bolted. Ed felt a terrible pain in his neck as he was jerked from the saddle into the air and . . .

Ed was jerked awake as the freight car came to a stop. He heard children crying. There was the stench of urine and excrement and moans of hunger and thirst. The boxcar was filled with men, women and children jammed together.

As the car jerked again to a full stop, Ed heard shouts of "Juden raus!" The doors slid open with a bang. Ed jumped down along with the other people. Men assisted women, who in turn helped the children. Jack-booted burly guards in grey uniforms herded the people into a ragged line. The guards carried long truncheons, which they used to keep the people moving.

The group was marched through a large gate bearing the sign "Arbeit Macht Frei". The air had a terrible odor of burning flesh. Now, Ed began to realize with growing horror where he was and where they planned on taking him.

The people were forced into a large building. A stentorian voice from a speaker announced: "You will all now be given showers while we delouse your clothing. After that, you will be fed. Undress completely and place your clothing in a neat pile so you can identify it later."

"Wait," Ed shouted. "There is some mistake. I'm not a J—, I am not Jewish." He was ignored. Ed and the people began to undress and soon everyone was naked. The women made vain efforts to cover their breasts and private parts.

"Schnell, schnell," barked the guards. A few guards leered and pointed their truncheons at some of the young women.

The group was driven into a large room. Ed estimated there were fifty or sixty of them. The room had a cement floor with drains and on one wall about a dozen showerheads protruded. Now Ed knew these showerheads were never intended to produce water.

A large metal door slammed, and there was the sound of a bolt being slid shut. Gas began to issue from the showerheads. There were cries, moans and screams. Some of the people clawed and pounded on the metal door. The gas stung Ed's eyes, and he started to choke. As he lost consciousness, he fell down to the cement and . . .

Ed walked along a cement sidewalk. It was early in the morning, and he felt fine. He wore business attire, carried a briefcase, and was on his way to check the books of a small company. Ed was not sure of the company's name or address, but as he reached the North Tower of the World Trade Center, he realized this was his destination. He walked into the building and took the elevator to the 95th floor. His ears felt the pressure change as the elevator swept upward. He got out and walked down the hall, stopping at a door. He checked the name on the door. Yes, this is the place.

Inside, he gave his card to the receptionist who studied it for a moment, then smiled. "Good Morning, Mr. Parker. Please have a seat. Mr. Fine will be with you shortly."

Ed sat in a comfortable leather chair. He had not slept well the previous night. He dimly remembered bad dreams, something about a sinking ship, a cell, and Nazi guards. A fresh copy of the New York Times lay on the table. The date read: Tuesday, September 11, 2001. Ed checked his watch. It was 8:30 and . . .

PHEROMONES

A young man wearing the short white jacket of a medical student stood facing the elevator in the basement of the medical school. It was nine o'clock on a Friday evening and most of the staff had gone home. A nurse approached, nodded a pleasant good evening to the young man and pressed the call button. When the elevator door opened, the student followed the nurse and stood behind her. She appeared to be in her late twenties. Her white uniform failed to hide her svelte figure. The student took a small glass vial with a spray attachment from his pocket and sprayed an odorless invisible mist toward the nurse. She took no notice, but after a few moments, she turned to face the student. She smiled at him, moved close and placing her arms around his neck, kissed him on the lips. On reaching the top floor, the elevator stopped, and the door opened. The nurse stood back and regarded the student in confusion, a deep blush suffusing her face.

"I'm terribly sorry," she stammered. "I don't know what came over me—I'm so embarrassed." She hurried away.

Another student waited outside the elevator.

"How did it go, Martin?" he asked.

"It worked even better than I hoped. She was ready to jump into bed with me."

Even from early childhood in Lucerne, Martin Gelzer showed signs of curiosity and intelligence. His father, a small shopkeeper who sold clocks and watches, encouraged him. Martin grew up to be a handsome young man, six feet in height with blond curly hair and piercing blue eyes. At the university in Zurich, he was popular, sociable and had no trouble finding female companionship. Martin did well, showed an interest in medicine and entered the medical school there.

During his last year of medical school, Martin was fascinated by an article about pheromones—chemicals purported to act as powerful sexual attractants in insects, mammals, and even humans. Martin learned these pheromones were present in the axillary sweat glands of men. He began to experiment. He was pleased to observe an apple rubbed in his armpit and then offered to girls he knew, often caused them to become amorous.

Martin persuaded a few of his classmates to form a company to research, produce, and possibly sell pheromones. He obtained samples of sweat from the armpits of virile male patients. Eventually he was able to identify and extract the most active components. This odorless substance produced sexual excitement in women within a short time after they inhaled it.

While on a skiing vacation at Davos, Martin's attention was caught by a beautiful young woman. He learned her name was Susan Kennedy, and she was American. At dinner she appeared in sexy après-ski attire catching the eye of everyone.

Susan Kennedy came from a wealthy Philadelphia family. After graduating *cum laude* from Wellesley College, she went on to earn an MBA from Harvard before moving to New York. Using starter money supplied by her family, Susan formed a venture capital company, and in time, invested in several start-up companies, which soon became successful. She was an accomplished swimmer, tennis player and skier. Although she had several men friends, Susan avoided romantic entanglements, preferring to spend her time building her company.

Martin wanted to meet her. He was an expert skier and introduced himself, offering to show Susan his favorite runs. His charming manner impressed her, she accepted his offer, and soon they were skiing and dining together. Susan was delighted to spend time with this handsome Swiss doctor. His daring on the slopes excited her as he led her down trails she would never have attempted alone. She found him to be considerate and affectionate. For his part, Martin suppressed an urge to become intimate with her, hoping instead to interest her in his business. Susan was intrigued when Martin described his company to her, but expressed skepticism about pheromones.

"Do they actually work, Martin?"

He assured her they did. They discussed the possibility of a business arrangement—her investing in his company. Martin realized with Susan's financial backing, his business could expand and prosper. They agreed he would fly to New York in a month.

On his arrival in New York, Martin checked into a hotel, shaved, showered and phoned Susan.

"Welcome to New York," she said, "if you're not too tired, we could meet for dinner. I know a great place."

"Fine," Martin said. "Where?"

Susan gave him the address of an upscale restaurant. "Is eight o'clock okay?" she asked.

Martin unpacked the small glass vial with its sprayer containing his most potent preparation. Tonight he planned to demonstrate his product, convince Susan it really works, and perhaps even get her into bed with him.

Martin took a taxi to the restaurant and told the Maitre d' he was expected. He was shown to a table, ordered a glass of wine, and waited for Susan. She appeared in a few minutes, looking radiant.

"Hi, Martin," she said. She kissed him on the cheek and sat down next to him.

"How was the flight?" she asked. "I'm glad you came."

"The flight was fine. It's good to see you again, Susan." She smiled, and Martin felt a warm glow anticipating an amorous evening.

"I hope you're hungry," she said. "The food here is terrific."

They ordered Oysters Rockefeller, followed by roasted quail and a dry white wine. While they ate, Martin surreptitiously removed the glass vial from his pocket. He waited until Susan's attention was diverted, causing her to turn her head and look away. Martin acted swiftly and was able to give a few sprays before Susan looked back at him. She never noticed. A few moments later, Susan stopped eating. She turned to face him, laid down her knife and fork and smiled at him lasciviously.

"You sprayed me with your pheromones, didn't you?" she said with a twinkle in her eye. "It wasn't necessary. Now, I really feel turned on, but not for you, lover boy. I guess you didn't know I'm gay?" Susan got up from the table. "I can't wait to get home to my partner."

Martin stared at her in disbelief.

"By the way," she called back as she walked away, "I think we can do business."

REALITY CHECK

Charles Goodman sat in front of his computer gazing at the blank screen. Nothing. Not even a screen saver. Charles was a writer of short stories and right now, he needed a story. He needed it like an addict needs a fix. "That's a cliché," he said to no one in particular.

If I had a story, he thought, I could send it to a contest at the Institute. What Institute? He thought. Oh, there is always an institute, and they usually have a contest.

Charles was determined. I know I can do it. I will start with a character. I will call him Tom. Charles typed "Tom" on the computer. There, he thought, that's a start. Now who and where is Tom? I will place him in England, at Cambridge. Yes, he is a student at Cambridge, an undergraduate. I will make it a warm spring day, just like here. Tom is wearing shorts and a polo shirt. Charles typed this in. He is walking down the lawn to the river, the Cam. Students are boating—they call it punting.

I need another character, Charles thought. A girl. I will call her

Pamela. He typed her in. Pamela is also a student and she knows Tom.

I need some dialogue now.

"Hi, Tom," Pamela greeted him. Charles typed it in. "What are you up to, Tom?" Charles typed.

"I'm just taking a stroll down to the river," Tom told her. They walked together, Charles typed.

"You look troubled, Tom," Pamela said. "Is something bothering you?"

"Yes," Tom said. "Something is wrong, dreadfully wrong. My wristwatch tells me it is eight-thirty, yet it is still light out and the sun is high in the sky."

"What does that mean?" Pamela asked.

"I had this weird thought," Tom answered.

"Tell me," Pamela said.

"I got this idea I might not be real. I—we could just be fictional characters in something someone is writing."

"You're right, that is weird," Pamela said.

"I mean, how can we tell? How can we prove it?" Tom asked. Tom and Pamela reached the river's bank, Charles typed.

"Look, I'll prove it," Pamela said. She recognized a fellow student punting on the Cam, Charles typed.

"There's Harry," Pamela said. "Hello, Harry," she called.

"Hi, Pamela," Harry responded.

"See, that proves it. If we were fictional characters, how could

Harry answer?"

"That doesn't prove anything," Tom said. "The Author could have typed that in. I have an idea, maybe, if there is an Author, we, or at least I, could contact him, her or it."

"You mean like a prayer?" Pamela asked.

"Whatever," Tom said. "I'm going to try it."

"I'm getting frightened," Pamela said.

"Are you there, Author?" Tom called.

"Yes, I'm here," Charles typed.

"What are you called?" Tom asked.

"I'm Charles," he typed.

Pamela began to cry. “Please stop it, Tom!” Pamela cried.

Tom ignored her. “I heard a strange story in philosophy class today,” Tom said.

“Tell me about it,” Charles typed.

“It took place many years ago,” Tom said. “This young professor was giving a public lecture. He was explaining how the Earth was a round ball floating in space. A woman interrupted him. That’s nonsense, the woman said. Everyone knows the world is flat and is supported on the back of a huge turtle. Then what is the turtle standing on? The professor asked. You are clever, young man, the woman said, but everyone knows it is turtles all the way down.”

“What does that mean?” Charles typed.

“It means,” Tom told him, “that you, Charles, the Author, could also be a fictional character.”

Charles felt his mouth go dry. “I’ve had enough of this,”

Charles said aloud and hit the delete key. The screen went blank. Then

Charles heard loud laughter seeming to come from above. He felt panic rising in his chest. Charles looked up and shouted, “Please, I want to live. Please don’t delete. I want . . .”

BOOKWORM

On a warm morning in September, a young man emerged from a subway station in lower Manhattan and walked along for several blocks. He paused at a delicatessen, purchased a sandwich and a Coca-Cola, before continuing. Several blocks later, he arrived at his destination, a store bearing the sign *Reader's Nook, New and Used Books.* He unlocked the door and entered, turning on the lights and changing the "closed" sign to read "open."

Martin Shaffer had been an avid reader since childhood. An only child, he lived with his parents in a modest apartment in Brooklyn. Uncle Emanuel, his father's brother, was Martin's only relative. Martin's uncle, the former owner of the *Reader's Nook,* provided Martin with an endless supply of reading material. Uncle Emanuel always dressed well and took a vacation every year. He was a widower and had a Japanese personal servant, Aoto, who was his constant companion. Martin remembered his father telling him Uncle Emanuel had saved Aoto from imprisonment during World War II when the FBI swept up every Japanese in the country to intern them in camps. Martin recalled visits to the bookstore on Saturdays. Uncle Emanuel showed him old books and read stories to him. Plato, the old cat who always sprawled on the desk in the small office, was invariably present. From time to time, as he grew older, Martin wondered how the small bookstore could support Uncle Emanuel's lifestyle.

Martin attended Fordham University, graduating with a major in English Literature. By the time he finished college, he had read most of the English and French classics. Martin dated a few women during the four years without a serious romance. His first job was as a copy editor for a small magazine and lasted for five years until the magazine folded. The search for another position ended when Uncle Emanuel conveniently died leaving the *Reader's Nook* to Martin. The day after Uncle Emanuel's funeral, Aoto disappeared never to be seen again. The rent and taxes for the bookstore were not exorbitant, and Martin decided to give it a try. The bookstore had a small, but faithful clientele, there were no employees, and for three years, Martin was able to operate and show a small profit. He lived on in his parents' rent-controlled apartment after their deaths.

The morning was relatively slow with only a few customers and at noon Martin retired to the miniscule office in the rear of the store. He retrieved his ham and Swiss on Rye from an insulated bag, opened his Coke, and settled back to eat. His eyes wandered over shelves of dusty old books when they landed on a volume he had never previously noticed. He took it down and examined it. The book was bound in smooth calf leather with a gold imprinted title reading *Memoir.* Underneath was author's name *Landow.* The binding was cracked in a few places. Martin opened the book noting it had been published in London in 1860. This piqued his curiosity because he always valued, but never could afford, antique books and first editions. He turned to the first chapter and began to read.

My name is Samuel Landow. I am writing this to record how I, an innocent young man, became entangled with an evil group of criminals to barely escape with my life.

At the age of 17, I was matriculated at Cambridge University. During the Christmas holiday of 1832, I went down to London with a few friends. On a lark, we made the rounds of pubs and grog shops, sampling the brews at each. Later in the evening, having drunk more than I could hold, I lost consciousness. I awakened to find myself on the floor of an ill smelling place, which proved to be the forecastle of a vessel. I rose and with an aching head, demanded of a seaman to know where I was and how I had gotten there. His reply was a snarl and a blow, with his fist, to the side of my head, which knocked me down. Eventually, I learned I had been "shanghaied" and spirited aboard this ship to work. The vessel was bound for the

Caribbean Sea on a voyage intended for piracy. I was forced to labor along with the rest of the crew. For sustenance, we lived on moldy ship biscuit.

After surviving several violent storms during which our ship was severely buffeted when I believed we would surely sink, we finally arrived into warm weather and calm seas. One night, our ship sailed into the harbor of a small island. A number of the crew quietly rowed ashore. Hours later, they returned drunk carrying money they had looted and boasting of how they waylaid passersby, beaten, and robbed them. We weighed anchor and left the harbor before daybreak. This behavior was continued week after week, going from island to island bringing back gold and other valuables. After a month or so, it was decided to hide our treasure somewhere and then continue our piracy. By this time I was more or less accepted as a member of the crew.

One night, we sailed into the harbor of an island whose name I disremember only that it sounded like the name of a famous Dutch painter. We carried our treasure, sealed in a wooden chest, into the long boat and rowed it ashore. While the rest of the crew searched for a suitable hiding place, I managed to slip away, hoping to escape. I hid in what appeared to be a charcoal pit. Some hours later I heard the sounds of the crew searching for me, infuriated and cursing. Eventually they gave up, rowed back to the ship, and sailed away. When dawn came, I identified myself to some of the residents, many of whom were Negroes. I did not tell them of the treasure. They treated me kindly offering me food and a place to rest.

Weeks later I was able to reach the island of St. Thomas. I described our pirate vessel to the authorities and a war ship was dispatched to find them. Following a brief battle, the pirate ship was burned, and the captives returned to St. Thomas where they were hanged.

Martin continued to read the brief story in which the author related how he finally was able to return to England. The idea of treasure hidden on a Caribbean island intrigued him. A quick computer search of the many Caribbean islands revealed a multitude of names. What famous Dutch painter could Samuel been referring to? The first one Martin thought of was Anthony Van Dyck. Sure enough, among the British Virgin Islands there was one name, Jost Van Dyke. Martin became excited and researched the island. It was a small one, only 4 square miles. Martin estimated Samuel Landow and the pirates had landed on Jost Van Dyke in 1833. At that time, the population consisted of a small number of whites, free people of color, and slaves who lived on plantations.

Maybe the treasure was still there? On an island so small it should be possible to search for it. Business was slow, and Martin had not had a vacation in three years. He decided he would go, and take two weeks, maybe more, to search for the treasure. Martin paid his bills in advance, placed a sign, "Closed for vacation", in the door and booked a flight for St. Thomas.

Arriving in St. Thomas, Martin knew he needed to take a ferry to Jost Van Dyke. He inquired at the airline counter and was referred to their travel consultant, Susan Landow.

Ever since she was a little girl, Susan Landow was different from her companions. She was a free spirit, not interested in marriage, housewifery, or children. At Bennington College in Vermont, she took courses in music, painting, English literature and Spanish. She was a pretty girl, not beautiful, with dark wavy hair and a slim feminine figure. During her obligatory work semester, she managed to wangle a position in the Travel Department of American Airlines. Susan learned quickly and was well liked because of her friendly disposition.

After graduation, Susan was able to get a regular job with American Airlines. After a period of training, she was sent to St. Thomas to be the airlines' travel consultant.

Martin started to ask her about the ferry to Jost Van Dyke when he noticed the nametag she wore. "Susan Landow," he said. "I just finished reading a book by a Samuel Landow. Any relation?"

"He was my great-grandfather," Susan said. "I knew he wrote a book, but I was never able to find a copy."

"Not surprising, it was a small edition. As far as I know, only 200 copies were ever printed. Do you know anything about the story?" Martin asked.

Susan shook her head. "No, I don't know anything about the book. Could you tell me about it?"

"Sure. Tell you what. It's lunchtime. Let's have lunch together, and I will tell you about the story."

Susan looked at him critically for a moment, then smiled and said "Okay let's go, I know a good place."

Together they left the small terminal and found her car, a Volkswagen Beetle.

"I haven't seen a VW bug like this in a while," Martin said.

"They're popular here. They don't burn much gas, and gas is expensive."

Susan drove to a small restaurant where they ordered lunch. Martin told her about the story. Susan became excited.

"Pirates! And treasure. Are you planning to search for it?" she asked.

"Yes. I'm going to try. I think it might be on Jost Van Dyke." He told her what Samuel Landow had written.

"I want to come! Please take me with you. I'll pay my own way. I can help. I know my way around the islands."

"Have you ever been to Jost Van Dyke?" he asked.

"No, but four eyes are better than two." She looked at him hopefully.

"Okay, and if we find anything, we'll split it. After all, it was your great-grandfather who told us about it."

Susan booked a room for them at the Sandcastle Hotel on Jost Van Dyke. "It's the only available room on the island," she told Martin, "so we'll have to share. I hope that's okay with you?" Martin nodded. His thoughts were on the treasure.

Martin and Susan took the ferry to Tortola and from there, the ferry to Jost Van Dyke. The Great Harbour, one of the busiest ports, was filled with yachts and other small commercial vessels. Many of the yachtsmen slept onboard their crafts and swam in to enjoy the beachside bars.

Their room was spacious in a private cottage with a king-size bed and a daybed. A sign in the bathroom amused Martin.

Caribbean Golden Rule: In this land of sun and fun, we never flush for number one.

"You can have the bed," Martin said. "I'll take the daybed."

"No, we'll take turns," Susan said.

They studied Samuel Landow's book and a printout of a Google Earth satellite view of Jost Van Dyke.

"Samuel wrote he heard the pirates talking about caves off the ends of the beaches," Martin said.

Martin and Susan rented a small boat with an outboard motor and spent hours touring the northeast shore of the island. They noticed at the ends of some of the beaches, the mountain, with many caves, came right down to the sea. Susan had brought a mask, snorkel, and fins. They took turns exploring cave after cave, one snorkeling in while the other stayed with the boat.

They took their meals at the Soggy Dollar, the hotel's restaurant. Martin slept on the daybed the first night. The following night, Susan took her turn there. An hour after the lights were turned off, she walked to the bedside. "Move over, Martin. Way over. That daybed is awful. I don't know how you managed to sleep on it." Martin chuckled and complied before falling asleep.

One day followed the next. Despite their liberal use of sun block, both were burned after a week of searching.

"There must be hundreds of caves," Susan said. "We could look forever and never find it."

Each night Martin searched through Samuel's book, hoping to find a clue. Then a single sentence! *"Let's put it near that big cock," one of the pirates had said, referring to a large rock which indeed resembled an erect male organ.*

The next day they cruised around looking for unusual rock formations. By mid afternoon they were getting discouraged. Then Susan yelled, "I see it! There it is."

Martin turned the boat and looked where she indicated. There was a rock formation resembling an erect phallus at the entrance of a small cave. They both got out of the boat and began to dig in the sand with their hands, while keeping hold of the anchor line.

After only a few minutes, Martin said, "there's something down here." Twenty minutes later they had cleared a small chest. Excitedly they removed enough sand from the lid so the two of them were able to pry it open. It was empty! They spent another half hour clearing the sand from the bottom of the chest only to find a plastic mailing tube. Inside the tube there was a small card, encased in plastic reading:

Pussycat, Pussycat, where have you been?
I've been to London to visit the Queen.
Pussycat, Pussycat, what did you there?
I frightened a little mouse under her chair.
E.S.

Martin and Susan looked at each other with a mixture of confusion and exasperation.

"What does that mean?" Susan asked.

Martin shrugged, "I haven't the slightest idea."

They sat in dejected silence for a few moments. "Well," Martin said in disgust. "It looks like someone beat us to it. Let's get out of here."

Back in their room they showered, went out for dinner, and bought a large bottle of Myers rum and a liter of pineapple juice. Back in the room, they consoled each other lubricating their misery with liberal libations of rum. By the time the bottle was empty, they were on the bed in each other's arms before passing out.

In the morning, with king-sized headaches, they dressed in silence, not looking at each other. Over coffee, they heard hurricane warnings on the radio.

Martin took the card with the Pussycat rhyme out of his pocket, studied it for a minute or so, then put it away. "There's something strange about this, but I don't know what it is. Anyway Susan, you still have a week of vacation left. Why not come back to New York with me? We can see a few shows, take in a concert, and eat in some fine restaurants. What do you say?"

She looked at him quizzically for a moment wondering what his motives were. "Okay, why not."

Back in New York, Susan moved into Martin's apartment. Although there was another bedroom, she chose to join Martin in his bed. The weather was typical of a beautiful New York fall, and they spent the next few days enjoying themselves. Martin continued to ponder over the rhyme. He began to piece things together, and then it hit him.

"I think my uncle was the one who discovered the treasure. The "E.S." on the card were his initials—Emanuel Shaffer. He must have read Samuel's book years ago. Maybe he and Aoto brought the treasure back here?"

"That's incredible," Susan said. "How could your uncle get it back here, through customs and all that?"

"I'll bet with Aoto's help, they emptied the chest and then the wily old gentleman chartered one of the commercial yachts with some of the treasure, and sailed it back to New York. They could have gone right up the Hudson, at night, to a marina, called a taxi and . . . now where would he have stashed it? He certainly wouldn't have hidden it in his apartment. He must have hidden it in the . . . come on Susan, let's go!"

The subway ride to Manhattan seemed to take forever. They rushed to the bookstore.

"I remember there was a cat," he told Susan, "and there's only one chair in the store."

The chair in the office rested on a small threadbare rug. Martin moved the chair aside, pulled the rug away to reveal a two-foot square trapdoor in the floor. He was able to pry it open exposing steps going down to a small dark room. Susan followed him down, and there it was! A large leather sack, like the mailbags carried by postmen, was filled with gold coins. He and Susan tried to lift it. He guessed it was about 60 pounds. At $1200 an ounce—close to a million dollars!

What would they do now? Well, that's another story.

ATALANTA REDUX

Whom the gods would destroy, they first make mad.

Medea, Euripides, 431 B.C.E.

At precisely 8:00 a.m., Jonathan Aldrich opened the door of his mansion and started down the walk where his limousine waited. The driver held the rear door open for him when Corliss appeared, breathless from her morning run.

"Good morning, Daddy," she said, kissing him on the cheek. "Have a lovely day."

She turned and walked to the front door. Jonathan watched his daughter, dressed in a jogging outfit, as she disappeared into the house.

En route to his office, Aldrich mused about his daughter, recalling how his late wife had chosen their daughter's name after her favorite radio character. Corliss was their only child. He pondered her future before turning his thoughts to today's activities.

A product of Princeton University and Harvard Law School, Jonathan Aldrich had done well. After years as a successful corporate attorney, he opened his own law practice, which in time grew to become one of the most prestigious in the city. He now employed dozens of young lawyers, many of them from the best law schools, who worked long hours hoping to achieve partner status.

Corliss showered, dressed in an outfit that did little to conceal the feminine charms of her slender, athletic form. She examined her face in the mirror to ensure there were no blemishes. Tall, blonde with blue eyes, Corliss was a natural beauty. She went downstairs to be served a light breakfast before leaving for her office. Corliss declined her father's frequent offers of a ride, insisting she needed to become independent.

Corliss had always been a runner. In high school she made the track team, excelling at the 440-yard dash. Corliss never lost a race. However, she behaved with such hauteur, most of her fellow students considered her to be stuck-up. Nevertheless, every boy in the school wanted to date her.

At college, her beauty attracted many male students, but she seldom dated the same one more than a few times because they always fell in love with her and wanted to possess her. One incident marred Corliss' college life. At a fraternity party someone drugged her drink. She awoke hours later to find her panties had been pulled off and a drunken sophomore attempting to have sex with her. Frightened and angry, she repulsed him, but for a long time thereafter she refused any sexual overtures.

Corliss distinguished herself as the only member of the women's track team who had never been beaten. For a time, she considered joining the U.S. Olympic Team and easily beat all the other applicants. Offered a position on the Olympic Team, she declined. Corliss decided she would rather gain recognition as an individual than a team member.

After graduation, at 21, Corliss considered law school, but eventually she settled on a position as a legal secretary in her father's law office. Many of the young men who worked for her father wanted to date her, but she regarded such offers with disdain. Corliss felt as "the boss' daughter" she would be quite a catch.

Corliss remembered how her brief relationships almost always culminated with a proposal of marriage. She propounded a plan to her father.

"Look Daddy, if one of your aspiring young associates wants to marry me, he must be able to beat me in a race. If he is able to beat me, I'll marry him, but if he doesn't, you have to fire him."

"That's ridiculous," Jonathan said. "What does beating you in a race have to do with marriage, and besides, why would I want to fire a competent young man just because he can't run fast? It's not fair."

Corliss persisted and insisted, so Jonathan, ever the lawyer, agreed to a compromise. "Okay, but you must wait until the young man proposes marriage before you explain your bizarre conditions. If he fails to win, he agrees to resign from my firm, and finally he must sign an agreement to hold me and my firm harmless in any event." Corliss nodded assent. "Tell me, Corliss," Jonathan, once again the father, asked, "what is the point of this? Do you think you are someone special?"

"Yes, Daddy, I believe I am."

Over the next several years, a number of third year-associates in Jonathan's law firm dated Corliss. Ten young men asked for her hand in marriage. Two of these withdrew their proposals when presented with the unusual conditions and resigned to find promising positions in other law firms, but eight young men agreed to the race. Each one lost and had to leave the firm. Word of Corliss' strange pre-conditions for marriage got out, and the number of suitors declined to zero. Corliss was now 30, still in peak condition but lonely. She had not had a date in over a year.

Derek Conroy was a third year associate. He had attended Brown University where he made the track team and was considered an excellent tennis player. At Yale Law School he made Law Review. His performance at the firm was exemplary. Jonathan planned to make him a partner.

Corliss had seen Derek a few times when he went to see Jonathan. On those occasions he nodded and gave her a faint smile on his way to the inner sanctum. This day, Derek and Jonathan came out of the inner office and together approached her desk.

"I don't believe you've met my daughter," Jonathan said to Derek. "Corliss, this is Derek Conroy. He and I will dine together this evening to celebrate his becoming a partner. I hope you'll be able to join us."

Corliss smiled. "Congratulations, Mr. Conroy. I'd be delighted to join you."

At dinner that evening, Corliss had time to admire Derek. In addition to his rugged good looks, she liked the way he interacted with her father. He was not subservient but spoke to the older man as an equal. The men had discussed the political situation in Washington. Over coffee, Derek declined a cigar but accepted a brandy. He turned to Corliss, "The Boston Pops will be giving a performance here tomorrow evening. Would you like to come with me to hear them?"

Corliss wondered whether her father had engineered this invitation, but she dismissed the thought. "Why yes, Mr. Conroy. I'd be delighted to join you," she said with a smile.

Corliss enjoyed the concert and Derek's company. A few days later he phoned her at home and invited her to dinner. Corliss was pleased and surprised. If the concert had been her father's doing, this dinner invitation probably was spontaneous. He took her to a small Irish pub.

"This is one of my favorite places to dine," Derek told her. "It's not pretentious, and the food is good."

The friendly bartender recognized Derek. "Good evening, Mr. Conroy. I have a booth just waiting for you and the lovely lady." Irish music played in the background.

"The shepherd's pie here is excellent," Derek said, when they were seated. "Would you like to try it?"

Corliss nodded eagerly. "Sure."

"I can also recommend my favorite ale."

"I don't usually drink beer, but if you recommend it, I'll try some."

The waiter came and took their order including two bottles of Newcastle Brown Ale.

Corliss enjoyed the dinner and the ale. Their conversation touched on her interests, and there were no references to office affairs. When he took her home, he said, "I hope we can see each other again soon."

"I'd like that," she said.

Derek called her once or twice a week. He took her to dinner, movies, a baseball game, and they shared a picnic on a warm Sunday afternoon. Once a week they went dancing. Corliss loved to dance, and Derek proved to be an excellent dancer. He held her close when leading, but he also permitted her the freedom to do her own steps. Corliss liked him more and more. From time to time, she wondered whether her father encouraged Derek, but as their relationship deepened, she realized she did not care. Recently, Derek began to kiss her on the cheek when saying goodnight, but soon his kisses moved to her lips. One night he drew her close and kissed her. Corliss put her arms around him and returned his kiss with fervor. She dreamed of losing her virginity in his arms. The next evening, in Derek's apartment, he started to make love to her. Corliss told him she loved him, but pleaded with him to be patient. She told him about the college episode.

Corliss and Derek saw each other every evening. Derek said he loved her and wanted to marry her. She did not know what to do. Corliss wanted to marry him, but was certain he knew about the peculiar prerequisite. Should she mention it? If she did, Derek might decline. Corliss felt she had to adhere to the practice. After all, if Derek loved her, he should be willing to risk his career. In the end, Corliss decided her personal pride demanded it, and she told him about the requirement.

Derek smiled when she told him. He readily agreed to the race and signed the "hold harmless" agreement. They scheduled the race for the following Sunday afternoon.

Sunday was a warm, sunny day in September. The course was about a mile and a half, on a level trail leading through a patch of woods and a meadow. The finish line was a tape stretched across the trail. At 2:00, Jonathan walked over to the finish line without enthusiasm and, after checking his watch for the desired starting time, fired a pistol into the air.

Both runners started and for a time were neck and neck. Corliss' mind was in turmoil. He is fast, but I think I can beat him. If I do, I have lost him. Should I hold back and let him win? Can I do it without him knowing?

Corliss, running as fast as she could, began to pull ahead of Derek. Both runners left the woods, and Corliss could see the tape of the finish line at the end of the meadow. At that moment her foot caught in a root, and she sprawled headlong with a scream.

Derek stopped and rushed over to her. She had fallen on her face, which was now bloody. He freed her foot from the root and turned her over. Corliss moaned and writhed in pain. Derek tried to reassure her while reaching for his cell phone. He dialed 911 requesting an ambulance. He picked her up in his arms and carried her toward the finish line where Jonathan waited.

At first, when Jonathan saw them come into sight, he threw up his hands, palms outward as if to inquire what was wrong. When they came closer, and he saw her bloody face, he shouted, "What happened?"

"She fell," Derek managed to gasp with the exertion of carrying her and running.

Jonathan rushed over as Derek laid her gently on the ground. Corliss was in great pain and barely conscious.

"I called for an ambulance," Derek said.

The ambulance came in a few minutes. A paramedic and an EMT came out and rushed over with a stretcher. They carried her back to the ambulance and, accompanied by Jonathan, roared off after telling Derek their destination. Derek followed the ambulance in his car.

At the hospital, they carried Corliss into the Emergency Room. The doctor on duty examined her, and she was given an injection of pain medicine. Although she appeared badly lacerated, her facial injuries proved to be superficial. Her face was cleaned up, several adhesive strips were applied, and she was taken for x-rays of her leg.

After examining the radiographs, the doctor went into the adjoining room where Jonathan and Derek waited. "Her foot has been badly mangled, her knee has been damaged, and at this point I can't tell whether her hip has been injured. I'm calling for an orthopedic consult. Meanwhile, we'll clean her up and try to make her comfortable with pain medication."

The orthopedic surgeon arrived in twenty minutes. He examined Corliss, who was sleepy, and called for CT scans and an MRI. After looking at the results, he told Jonathan and Derek, "Several bones are broken in her foot and ankle. She has a torn anterior cruciate ligament in her knee. The tissues holding her hip in place may also have been torn. She will need several operations. We can admit her here, and I can perform those operations, or we can arrange for a transfer to another institution when she has been stabilized."

"Can we see her now?" Jonathan asked.

"Yes, but just for a few minutes. She's groggy from the pain medication."

Jonathan arranged for Corliss to be transferred to the university hospital in the vicinity. This hospital had a large orthopedic department with an excellent reputation.

Over the next several years, Corliss underwent operations on her foot and knee, but the damage had been severe. She would never run or dance again. With luck, she would be able to ambulate with the aid of a walker or cane. Between the operations, Corliss stayed at a rehab center.

Derek visited almost every day, bringing flowers and a cheerful attitude. Their conversation soon turned to the race and the question of the winner.

"Let's assume that you won," Corliss told him, and, "if you still want me, I'll marry you."

They set a date for the wedding, but she developed an infection requiring an additional procedure and the wedding was postponed. Additional complications required more postponements, and as time went on, these postponements extended further and further into the future.

One day, when Derek visited Corliss at the rehab center, she appeared confused and did not recognize him. The nurses told him this confusion had been sporadic but ongoing for weeks. Derek told Jonathan, who arranged for a psychiatrist to visit Corliss. After a series of visits over a period of months, the psychiatrist gave Jonathan and Derek the grim news.

"It's some form of dementia," the psychiatrist told them. "It could be the result of a drug reaction, or a minor brain hemorrhage, or the onset of Alzheimer's. We will do some tests, but basically we will just have to wait and hope that it's temporary."

But it was not temporary. She was mostly wheelchair-bound but could get around with a walker. Jonathan brought her home and arranged for several women to provide full-time care for

Corliss. Three years later, Corliss had her 40th birthday. Jonathan, Derek, and a few friends attended, but Corliss could not recognize any of them.

Corliss lived another twenty-two years before she died, still chaste, but chased no longer. When Jonathan died, Derek took over the law firm.

NEVER LOOK A GIFT HORSE IN THE MOUTH

I always liked horses and rode whenever I had the opportunity and the money. Not that I was a great rider, but I enjoyed being in the saddle. At this time of my life, I was an assistant professor at the University of Vermont, College of Medicine.

One of my friends from the Department of Medicine stopped by my office one day to tell me that he had just acquired a horse. Dr. Kenneth Philips, a recent arrival from the Rockefeller Institute in New York, was interested in immunology. He planned to immunize the horse with a vaccine to study the horse's antibodies.

"That's great, Ken," I said.

"Would you like to see him?" he asked.

Lyric was a beautiful tall chestnut. He was the sole occupant of the small stable located just behind the medical school. I noticed "NYPD" tattooed on his left flank.

"He's beautiful," I said. "Can he be ridden?"

"Sure," Ken said. "Why not? The only thing I do with him is draw some blood every month."

"I'd like to ride him," I said.

"No problem, the exercise will do him good. The stable hand here has some tack that came with him."

I was anxious to become better acquainted with Lyric and ordered light trail shoes for him. The next day, I threw a halter around his neck, led him to the paddock that adjoined the stable, and turned him loose. I sat on the fence to watch. Lyric stood there for a minute taking in this new opportunity for exercise. He began to gallop around the corral emitting the loudest fart I ever heard each time he made a turn. I damn near fell off the fence with laughter. After five minutes of watching his musical progress, I jumped down and just stood there. Lyric galloped at me swerving only at the last minute scaring the hell out of me. The next time he came around, I didn't jump aside. I turned my back to him. He slowed to a walk, came up behind me, and shoved me with his head so that I stumbled. He kept shoving me.

The stable hand watched this performance. "He just wants to play with you," he said.

I learned that Lyric had other games. He would lie down in the corral and neigh. I was supposed to run over and try to keep him from getting to his feet. A horse needs to swing his head and neck in order to get up, but can be kept down by light pressure on his neck or head. Of course, he never let me get close enough to do that. As soon as I started to approach, he got up and galloped around the corral, farting in derision.

The following week I had him saddled and bridled and took him out for a walk along a dirt road leading to the countryside. His gaits were a pleasure. His trot was a delight requiring only gentle posting, and I let him canter for 100 yards or so. He responded to the slightest rein or leg pressure. *This will to be fun.* Little did I realize why Lyric no longer worked for the New York City Police Department.

As we walked past a meadow, some dairy cows noticed us and began to wander over to the fence. Lyric grew nervous. He was a city horse and mistrusted cows. He began to side-step and get as far away from the cows as possible. There was more to come.

A few days later, I took him for a morning walk and everything was fine until we came to a large pile of gravel. Lyric stopped. After clucking a few times and nudging him in the ribs with my heels, it was clear he wasn't going to pass that pile. I dismounted and with my hand on the bridle near his mouth tried to get him to walk with me. No go. He shook his head, his eyes grew wild, and he held his ground. Remembering something I had once seen in a movie, I took off my jacket and threw it over his head. He didn't like it, but I was able to lead him past the pile. The rest of the ride was uneventful.

I rode Lyric every morning before going to my office. *What luck to be able to ride this fine horse for free!* My good luck appeared to continue until one morning when we were walking past a construction site. A large excavator came to life and raised its huge "claw." Lyric reared, and I lost one stirrup, but managed to keep my seat. He turned, laid his ears back, and raced toward the stable at a full gallop. Maybe he got the bit between his teeth, but I couldn't stop him. We crossed a large field studded with chuckholes, and I expected to be killed. We approached a four-lane highway en route to the stable. The road filled with morning traffic. I tried to turn him away or stop him, but I could only cling to his mane. The cars in one lane had stopped for a traffic light. He ran straight at a car, leaping over the hood to cross the highway. My riding experience did not include jumping, but miraculously I was able to hold on. I'll never forget the horrified expression on the face of the woman driver as we sailed past her windshield.

Somehow we reached the stable. The stable hand came out as I managed to dismount. My knees were wobbly, and I shook uncontrollably.

"What the hell happened?" he asked, eyeing Lyric who foamed at the mouth and was breathing hard.

"That horse is neurotic," I said. "He needs a psychiatrist. He damned near killed me!"

The stable hand chuckled. "I told you he was nuts." *I didn't recall any such warning.* He led the sweating horse into the stable.

Now I knew why Lyric was here in Vermont. This big beautiful animal had been unfit for duty as a police horse. At least he could continue his service to humanity by making antibodies. As for me, I never rode him again.

EROS

Cynthia Jones sat in a classroom of New York University taking a course in European History. Gazing out the window she could see snowflakes falling. Looking around at the 30 some odd college students taking notes, and the youngish professor, Cynthia realized she was the oldest person in the class. She was 46.

Her thoughts went back to when she had been a senior at Barnard. Her thoughts drifted back to a party where she met Robert, a third year law student. They started to date, and by the time he had passed the Bar and graduated, they were engaged. Robert accepted a good offer from a law firm in Chicago, and she dropped out of college to join him. What followed was 24 years of a happy marriage with a son and a daughter grown and married. Then two years ago the horrible phone call from Robert's office telling her of his fatal heart attack.

Cynthia sold their home and returned to a small apartment in Greenwich Village. She had some women friends but was bored and decided to finish her Bachelors degree.

The professor continued to lecture. " . . . and so, in 1789, emboldened by the success of the American Revolution an irate, starving crowd in Paris, stormed the Bastille starting the reign of terror that was the French Revolution."

Cynthia found herself sitting at an outdoor café in Paris. It was April, the chestnut trees were blooming, and the day was warm. She watched the people as they walked by, waiting for someone. Cynthia did not know for whom she waited, but she had a happy, expectant air.

She saw him as he approached. He was tall, well dressed and handsome with a thin moustache. She decided his name must be Pierre. Moments later, as if conscious of her stare, he saw her and walked up to her table. He said something to her in French asking if he might join her. Cynthia smiled and with a shrug indicating she did not know a word of French, gestured for him to join her.

The man removed his hat and, calling over a waiter, ordered coffees for the two of them. He looked at her with delight as they sipped their coffee murmuring words she could not understand. After a time, Pierre took both of her hands, brought them to his lips and kissed them.

Cynthia had a warm feeling in her heart. She knew this was the man. She liked him a great deal and wanted to be with him.

An old man selling trinkets stopped at their table, offering his wares. Pierre stopped him, selected a broach, and with a smile, offered it to Cynthia. It was a silver cameo surrounded by tiny faux pearls. "Pour tu, cherie." She was charmed.

After perhaps a half an hour, he stood and indicated she should join him. Together they walked along the street. At first she took his arm holding it close to her body, but soon he had his arm around her waist.

They found themselves alone in a sunlit wood. Pierre led Cynthia to a grassy glade, took her into his arms and kissed her. She put her arms around his neck and drew him close. He kissed her again, this time biting her lower lip before his tongue darted in to touch hers. Cynthia became excited. He unbuttoned her blouse, lowered her bra and began to fondle her breasts. He kissed them and she felt her nipples become hard. Pierre unzipped her skirt, pulled it down around her ankles and continued kissing her around her navel. Cynthia was so aroused she could barely stand. He backed her against a tree, pulled off her panties and drew her hand to his erection, which protruded from his trousers. It felt immense, and she guided him to her. Cynthia could no longer keep her feet and together they fell on the grass. She experienced an overwhelming orgasmic sensation as he climaxed within her. He felt quite light as he lay on top of her as if he weighed almost nothing. After a few moments, he kissed her again and then was gone.

The professor finished the lecture. "So, eventually Napoleon became prominent, declared himself Emperor and for the next 20 or 30 years, France dominated most of Europe."

Cynthia left the class and walked back to her apartment. Her lower lip was swollen and assumed she had bitten it herself. Back in her apartment she cooked and ate dinner and spent the evening watching TV. She felt tired but relaxed. Cynthia decided to take a warm bath. As she undressed she was surprised to find a silver cameo, surrounded by tiny faux pearls, pinned to her blouse, and a few small leaves and blades of grass fell from her panties. She smiled and slept well that night.

SECOND CHANCES

James Johnson woke to the rich smell of frying onions and bacon. He knew his mother was cooking collards, but he asked, "What you cookin, Momma?"

"I'm cooking lion meat for dinner," she said. "Get your body out of that bed. You going to lose your job if you late."

Mikayla was a good cook. She worked weekdays cooking and cleaning for white families, but Saturdays she stayed home to catch up on her own cleaning, cooking, and laundry. Sundays she and James went to church.

Living in a tarpaper, sharecropper's shack in Georgia with Willie and their infant son, James, was not the life Mikayla wanted. She had managed to save some money and persuaded Willie to move north. They found a small apartment in the Crown Heights section of Brooklyn, New York where she hoped Willie would find work. In his search for a job, he stopped in local bars and often came home drunk. Some nights, Willie did not come home at all. Then, despite Mikayla's inquiries Willie disappeared, never to be seen again.

Crown Heights was largely a Jewish neighborhood with the Kol Israel Synagogue, Medgar Evans College and the headquarters of the Chabad-Lubavitch Movement. Other features of the neighborhood were the Bartholomew's Protestant Episcopal Church and Rectory and Ebbets Field, the stadium of the Brooklyn Dodgers. The Jews and Blacks avoided each other. The Jews patronized kosher markets and Jewish clothing stores while the Blacks shopped at other locations.

"Why they so different, Momma?" Mikayla sometimes worked for Jewish families. "I don't rightly know. All I can tell you is, they wear different clothes, and they don't eat pork. They all have two separate sets of dishes, pots and pans. And something else. The married women are bald as an egg. They shave they heads and wear wigs."

"That's weird," James said.

Mikayla shrugged, "It is what it is."

As James grew up, the neighborhood changed. More Blacks migrated from the South to find homes in Crown Heights. Whites sold out at a loss, and realtors made a profit from the Blacks.

James became accustomed to the voice of Red Barber on the radio announcing every game the Dodgers played at Ebbets Field. He became interested in baseball and the Brooklyn Dodgers. He got to know the names of many of the players. Roy Campanella, Gil Hodges, Pee Wee Reese and Duke Snider became familiar names. He often heard the name of Leo Durocher, the fiery manager of the Dodgers. There was seldom a game when Durocher failed to rush to the infield to argue violently with the umpire. Durocher got the nickname of "Leo The Lip".

James attended public school and two years of high school. During those years, Mikayla kept him out of trouble, forbidding smoking, alcohol, drugs, and gangs.

Mikayla didn't like it when he dropped out of high school to find work, but they needed the money. James found a job in a garage and learned to be an auto mechanic. He got to be one of the best in the garage. James became friendly with Clyde, a white man who owned the garage.

The Japanese attacked Pearl Harbor, and America was at war. Two years later, James was drafted into the Army. In those days, the military was segregated, and James was assigned to the 92nd Infantry Division, an all-black unit. In 1944, his regiment was deployed to Italy where it saw heavy combat in the Italian Campaign. After Germany surrendered, James was discharged and returned home. Clyde was glad to have him back at work.

James, like thousands of other African-American fans, became enthusiastic when Jackie Robinson joined the Brooklyn Dodgers. Jackie Robinson was the first Negro to play in the major leagues. When he showed up for the first game, several of the Dodgers decided they would not play with a Negro. On hearing this, Leo Durocher strode into the dugout and announced that he would guarantee that any player who refused to go out on the field would be banned for life from the major leagues. They all played. That season, Jackie Robinson was voted Rookie of the Year.

James often listened to the Dodger games on the radio while at work. When he had money to spare, he would buy a ticket for the bleachers at Ebbets Field and watch the game. At least half of the spectators were black.

Mikayla was ailing, but she still managed to get to church on Sundays. James often walked with her to the church and returned to take her home. She was frail, and he didn't want her to fall.

At church one Sunday morning, Mikayla was talking to two women when James appeared, and she introduced him. "This is my son James." He shook hands with the older woman.

"This is my daughter Chelsea," she said. Chelsea looked to be a few years younger, and James thought she looked sexy. She wore a short skirt and a blouse, making it obvious she hadn't been to church. Later at home, James asked his mother about Chelsea. "She is a good girl," Mikayla said. "She lives with her Momma. Works at a barbershop giving manicures. Call her up. Maybe you could take her out."

"Maybe I will," James said. That evening he called and spoke to Chelsea. After a brief conversation he asked whether she would like to go out with him. Chelsea agreed and the following Saturday, he took her to a movie. They had a good time. He asked her out again. James and Chelsea soon dated every Saturday night. He took her to movies, to dinner and dancing. Chelsea loved to dance. He wanted to take her to a Dodgers game, but she wasn't

interested in baseball. After they had dated for a year, James proposed to Chelsea. He was in love. He knew that she met many men in the barbershop and didn't want to lose her. Chelsea was delighted with the modest, diamond engagement ring James offered, and she accepted. James couldn't wait to tell his mother that he and Chelsea were engaged. Mikayla was pleased and started planning for the wedding. James and Chelsea got a marriage license. They were married in church by the pastor. James asked Clyde to be his best man. "Sure," he said, "I'll be glad to. I'll stick out like a sore thumb in that church, but I don't mind." Chelsea's mother walked her down the aisle, and the organ played the wedding march. Five of Chelsea's friends attended as bridesmaids. Afterwards, there was a reception at the rectory for more friends. Clyde brought his girlfriend. One of Chelsea's friends lent her apartment to the wedding couple so they could spend their first night together.

Chelsea moved in with James and Mikayla. The apartment was small with only one bathroom, and there was little privacy. Mikayla did not like cigarette smoke, and Chelsea was a smoker. Chelsea reluctantly agreed not to smoke in the apartment. Mikayla cooked the meals, and Chelsea continued working.

Five years later, James came home one night to find Mikayla on the floor. She had a heart attack. He called 911, and the ambulance took her to Kings County Hospital. When James arrived at the hospital, Mikayla was dead.

James and Chelsea now had the apartment to themselves. Chelsea smoked nonstop, though James didn't like it. Her girlfriends often came to visit. James bought a TV set and offered to play a Dodgers game for them, but none of Chelsea's friends were interested in baseball. He often spent Saturday afternoons and Sundays alone watching a game, while Chelsea went out with her friends.

In 1955 the Brooklyn Dodgers competed with the New York Yankees for the World Series Championship. Every fan in

Brooklyn was excited at the prospect that the Dodgers could win the championship. The winning game was played in Yankee Stadium. Mel Allen was the announcer. The Dodgers won four to three.

Chelsea began to come home later and later. There were times when James had to get his own dinner and some nights she didn't get home until he had gone to bed. On one night, James was awake when she got into bed.

"I met someone, James," she said. "You're a good man, but I don't want to be married to you anymore. I want a divorce."

James was quiet for a moment. "Okay by me," he said and rolled over to sleep. Chelsea moved her things out the next day. When the divorce papers came, he signed them. "It wasn't much of a marriage," he said, to no one in particular.

James was now alone. He still had his job and was free to watch all of the Brooklyn Dodger games. He volunteered several days a week after work coaching the boy's church baseball team. He also helped the younger kids with their homework. He told the children to stay away from drugs and alcohol.

In 1956, Jackie Robinson left the Dodgers because of physical ailments. During the ten years he was with the team, he had 1,518 hits, 137 of these were home runs with 734 RBIs. His batting average was .311. Jackie was entered into the Baseball Hall of Fame and his number, forty-two, was retired by all of the major leagues.

The following year, what happened was unbelievable to James and thousands of other fans. The Dodgers left Brooklyn to become the Los Angeles Dodgers. The Brooklyn Dodgers were no more. Three years later, as if as a memorial, Ebbets Field was demolished with apartment houses covering the area where the stadium once stood. The only evidence that the stadium had existed was a parking lot with a sign, "Ebbets Field."

The light had gone out of James's life. He didn't watch baseball anymore. He continued working at the garage, coaching the team, and helping the younger children at the church, but there was a gap in his life. On evenings when the weather was fair, James often strolled over to where the stadium had been and walked around the area. There were a few stone benches and sometimes he just sat until it grew dark, remembering the stadium filled with enthusiastic fans.

On one such evening he sat, remembering the ball games. He imagined he could hear the roar of the crowd. He opened his eyes. He could still hear the crowd. Where was it coming from? Then he heard the unmistakable crack of a bat sending the ball to the outfield and moments later, a baseball landed on the ground near him. Half believing it was real he picked it up. It was new baseball that had been signed by Jackie Robinson. He sat in astonishment massaging the ball.

"Excuse me," a voice said, "I guess you didn't hear me. I don't want to bother you. Is that a baseball you're holding?"

James turned to see a young woman sitting near him. He could see in the gloom that she was attractive.

"Yes, Ma'am, it is indeed a baseball. A Brooklyn Dodgers baseball."

"I love baseball," she said. "Too bad the Dodgers left Brooklyn."
"How about dinner and a movie with me tomorrow night?" he said.

She smiled. "Sure, we can talk about baseball." James felt something good was starting in his life.

A LION IN THE BRONX

Rebecca's first day at Brooklyn High School was confusing. She was nervous as she walked down a corridor filled with students. She stopped a young man to ask, "Excuse me. This is my first day, I'm not sure where to go." The young man smiled at her.

"Me, too. My first day, we'll go together."

He took her hand, guiding her through the mob of students. "My name is Dino. Dino Manelli."

"Rebecca, Rebecca Levine. Thanks for helping me."

In the days that followed, Rebecca and Dino often found themselves in the same class and sometimes, they went to lunch together.

Rebecca was the sole child of a rabbi, who led a small congregation in a local synagogue. His wife died years ago and he brought Rebecca up, teaching her the Sabbath prayers and stories from the Old Testament.

Dino's father was the proprietor of a popular pizzeria. His wife had died years ago, and he had brought up Dino and his two brothers in their apartment over the pizzeria.

By the end of the first school year, Dino and Rebecca were acquaintances. During the second year, they became friends, while recognizing that their relationship was a forbidden one. Dino was taught not to associate with non-Catholics, and Rebecca was ordered to shun Gentiles. By the third year, Rebecca and Dino were in love, and during their final year in high school, they somehow found the opportunity to consummate their love. By graduation, Rebecca was pregnant.

"We must tell our parents," Dino said, and Rebecca agreed. When she confessed to her father, he called her bad names in three languages, and threw her out of the house.

Dino's experience was no better. His father and brothers held a conference then announced, "Dino, you have brought shame on our family. Manelli's have never married outside of the Church." He handed Dino three thousand dollars.

"Take this and get lost. We never want to see your face again."

Dino and Rebecca were married in a civil ceremony. They had long ago decided that each would maintain their own religion and respect the other one's. They fled to the East Bronx, where they found a small apartment.

Dino found a pizzeria nearby that was going out of business. He was able to persuade a local bank to give him a loan to buy that restaurant. He and Rebecca cleaned it up, painted, and restored it, and then hung out a sign, "Manelli's Pizza." He knew exactly what to do. His father had taught Dino and his brothers the secrets of successful pizzas. The oven was in good condition, and Dino ordered flour, yeast, cheese, and the makings of a tomato sauce. Rebecca found two pictures depicting Italian scenes, and hung them on the walls. She worked with Dino until the baby was due. Dino hired an assistant.

It didn't take long for word to get out, and people came in to try the new place. The found the pies were better than anything they had previously experienced, thin crust, plenty of cheese, great sauce, and a variety of optional additions. Within six months, business prospered.

Rebecca gave birth to a boy, a strong, healthy infant. She named him Ari.

"What kind of name is that?" Dino asked.

"It's Hebrew. It means, 'Lion'."

"Ari Manelli. That's a good name," he said.

Ari was a healthy, husky infant. As he grew he became taller and larger than his playmates. When Ari entered the neighborhood public school, Rebecca, a gentle soul, exhorted him to "be a good boy." However, Ari soon gained a reputation as a prankster, responsible for dipping a girl's braids in paint during art class or throwing spitballs at the teacher when her back was turned. He was a mediocre student. In third grade, some of the children in Ari's class were unruly, writing graffiti on bathroom walls and vandalizing school property. Ari was often sent to the principle's office for fighting in the schoolyard, although investigation invariably revealed he was defending a younger, or smaller student against a bully.

Ari's parents, disturbed by reports of his behavior, transferred him to the parochial school. Dino knew the nuns were devoted teachers who demanded and maintained order in the classroom. Dino and Rebecca felt the tuition was money well spent.

While not distinguishing himself academically, Ari passed all of his subjects and ceased his unruly behavior. After four years, Ari graduated and entered St. Francis High School.

In high school, his large size and shyness discouraged relationships with classmates, and Ari did not have many friends. In his sophomore year, Ari joined the wrestling team and soon distinguished himself by winning many matches.

Ari was dismayed to learn his mother suffered from advanced cancer. As Rebecca lay dying, she called him to her bedside.

"Tobacco, alcohol and drugs are not good things. I want you to promise you will never smoke, drink, or use drugs."

"Mother . . . ," Ari started to say, with tears in his eyes, but his mother persisted.

"Listen to me. I have a feeling that if you do any of those things, something bad will happen to you. And one more thing. Don't let anyone cut your hair. I haven't much time. Promise me."

"I promise, Mother," Ari said.

His mother smiled, and a few hours later breathed her last.

Two gangs, the Muggers and the Addictos, dominated the neighborhood. The Muggers, most of whom were Italian, extorted protection money from the local stores and small businesses by threatening the owners that their premises would be damaged if they did not pay. Ari came to know some of the Muggers as acquaintances and became friends with one of them named Guido. The Addictos, an Irish gang, were far worse, and sold drugs like crack cocaine and crystal meth. They manufactured these drugs in a small factory located in a deserted warehouse.

On his way to school each day, Ari passed a neighborhood gym where men practiced boxing. Several times each month, boxing matches were held there. Ari wandered in one evening to observe two men sparring in the ring.

While he watched, an older man approached him. "You look like a strong lad. Would you like to put the gloves on with someone?"

Ari grinned. "I never did it before. I don't know how, but sure, I'll try it." The man helped Ari to put on boxing gloves and beckoned to a young man who watched the bout. "This is Collin," he said, "he'll spar with you. What's your name?"

"I'm Ari."

"Ari what?"

"Ari Manelli."

"What kind of name is Ari?"

"It's the Hebrew word for lion."

"Okay. Get in there and be a lion."

When the bout had finished, Collin climbed into the ring, and Ari followed. As Ari approached Collin in the center of the ring, he was greeted with a blow to his face rocking his head back.

"Keep your guard up," the older man called, but Ari did not understand. He tried to protect his face with both hands only to be peppered with blows to his body by Collin who danced around him.

"Hit him!" the older man shouted, and Ari tried to swing wide punches at his opponent, but Collin blocked them all. After a few minutes it was obvious Ari was taking a beating.

"Enough," the older man yelled and helped Ari out of the ring. "Look," he said, removing the gloves from Ari's hands, "you need some lessons. My name is Mike. Stop around some afternoon, and I'll give you some pointers."

"How much will it cost?"

"Don't worry about it," Mike told him.

Over the next few months, Ari stopped into the gym every afternoon after school where Mike introduced him to the art of pugilism. It did not take long for Ari to become a good boxer. He was able to withstand severe blows without much effect, and what he lacked in technique he made up with in strength and endurance. When Ari's blows connected, his opponents knew they had been hit and were often knocked to the floor. After a few more months, Ari won several matches and in the gym they began to call him "Ari the Lion." By his senior year, Ari, at 17, was a tall, muscular young man who commanded respect from those whom he met. Rumors of his strength percolated from the gym to the neighborhood. One story told of a neighbor who had a flat and had no jack. Ari was able to lift the rear quarter of the car so a new tire could be attached.

Following graduation Ari looked for employment. He started working at his father's pizzeria. Dino taught him everything about pizzas.

He worked in the kitchen from dawn to late at night, making the dough and stoking the oven.

Guido introduced Ari to a girl he knew. Gloria was a young woman who wore short skirts, low cut jeans and sleeveless, tight-fitting tops. Ari was soon smitten and before long they talked of marriage. Ari brought Gloria home to meet his father.

Afterwards, Dino said, "She hangs around with the Mugger gang. I saw her with them the other day. Surely you can find a nicer girl."

"She's okay," Ari said, "and I like her. She's the one I want."

His father shrugged. "Don't forget the promise you made to Mother."

A week later, a sudden major heart attack left Ari an orphan.

Ari and Gloria scheduled their wedding the next month. Guido was going to be his best man. A week before the wedding, Ari invited Guido and many friends to a party at the pizzeria. Most of them were Muggers whom Ari detested. The party became boisterous and the guests consumed a lot of beer.

Then Ari rose. "I have a riddle for you," he announced. "If you can tell me the answer, I will give each of you five dollars, but if you can't, you must each give me five dollars. What do you say?"

There was silence for a moment, and then most of them said, "Okay, let's hear it."

Ari told them the riddle. "A beggar had a brother who died. Yet the man who died had no brother. How can this be?" The group looked puzzled. "Come back here the day before the wedding with your answer," Ari told them as he and Gloria left the party.

That evening, Gloria asked Ari, "What's the answer?"

"I can't tell you," he said.

"Please, please," she pleaded.

"No, if they find out, I will have to pay a lot of money."

"I promise I won't tell anyone."

Ari finally gave in, but Gloria was more faithful to the Muggers than to her husband-to-be. The day before the wedding, when Ari met with the group in the pizzeria, he asked them for the answer.

"The beggar was a woman," some chorused. Others yelled, "He had a sister!"

Ari was enraged. He glared at Gloria. "You betrayed me, you bitch," he shouted. He took a wad of five-dollar bills from his wallet and threw them at the group. When they laughed and jeered, Ari picked up a peel, the large wooden paddle used to slide pies into the oven, and began to whale about him, striking the group, and knocking some down. Many of the wounded were able to escape, but some had to be taken to the hospital in ambulances. By the time police arrived, Ari was gone. No charges were ever filed because none of the victims dared complain. They feared Ari. The next day, Guido and Gloria were married.

Years passed. Ari continued working at the pizzeria. He led a quiet life and continued training at the gym, but matches were few. Those who climbed into the ring with him were invariably demolished. The Muggers all hated Ari, and they avoided any contact with him.

One day, a woman who entered the pizzeria attracted Ari's attention. She was tall, slender, with long hair and a figure accentuating her feminine attributes. When her dark eyes rested on Ari she smiled at him. He was overwhelmed. It had been years since he had been with a woman, and her beauty inflamed him, hotter than the fire of the oven.

The woman ordered a Hawaiian with ham, pesto, and extra pineapple. Ari made the pizza, boxed it, and his eyes followed her as she left the store. That night he dreamed about her. In the dream, she asked to see the pizza oven. He led her into the kitchen and embraced her while pizzas in the oven charred.

A week later, the woman returned. This time Ari took her order.

"Can you deliver it?" she asked.

"Certainly," he said. "Address and phone number?"

She smiled as she gave the information. "My name is Delia," she said in a sexy whisper. Ari sent his assistant to deliver the pizza.

That evening Ari phoned her. "My name is Ari," he said. "I saw you in the pizzeria today."

"How can I help you?" she asked.

"I'd like to see you again," Ari managed to say.

"Are you asking me for a date, Ari?"

"Yes, I am. How about Saturday night?" he asked, with his heart in his throat.

"What did you have in mind, Ari?" she whispered.

"I could pick you up at eight, and we could go somewhere nice for dinner."

"Mmm, I'd like that. See you at eight."

Saturday evening, Ari pressed her doorbell. Delia greeted him with a smile. She wore a black cocktail dress.

"Hi, Ari, come in." Her apartment was small, dark with a bedroom and a kitchen. Piano music played softly from a stereo, and Ari could smell the scent of her perfume.

"Are you ready to go?" Ari asked.

"I'm all set," she said taking his arm.

Ari took her to Dugan's Irish Pub, one of his favorite restaurants. The bartender recognized him.

"Good evening, Ari. Would you like a booth for you and the lady?"

Ari nodded, and the bartender showed them to a quiet booth towards the rear of the pub. Irish music played in the background.

"I can recommend the steaks here," Ari said.

The waiter arrived, and they each ordered filet mignon.

"How would you like yours, Miss?"

Delia smiled. "Rare. I'd like mine rare."

"And you, Sir?"

"Make mine medium rare, please."

"And to drink?" the waiter asked, looking at Delia.

"What kind of red wine do you have?" she asked.

"We have a merlot, pinot noir, and a cabernet sauvignon."

"I'll have the cab," Delia said.

Turning to Ari, the waiter asked, "And you, Sir?"

"Just a glass of water." The waiter left.

"Why aren't you drinking?" she asked.

"I don't drink alcohol," Ari told her.

Delia looked at him quizzically but did not ask the reason. She asked about the business at his pizzeria, and they chatted until their food arrived.

Ari and Delia were well into dinner when two men walked over to their booth and, ignoring Ari, began to talk to Delia as if they knew her. Ari was offended. He told them quietly, "The lady is with me. Get lost."

The men ignored him and continued to talk to Delia. Ari stood up and repeated, "I told you guys to get lost."

One of the men put his hand on Ari's chest, attempting to push him back. "Sit down, lad."

The push did not move Ari. The man might have been pushing a brick wall. Ari grabbed the man's arm and forced him to his knees. The other man turned and swung a fist at Ari. The blow never arrived. Ari blocked it and with his left arm, punched the man in the jaw, breaking it, and knocking him down. Ari then grabbed both men by their hair, and banged their heads together, leaving them both unconscious. He beckoned to the waiter.

"Get this trash out of here," he said. Two of the waiters dragged the unconscious men away. Ari resumed his seat and continued to eat.

Throughout this brief fracas, Delia reacted with surprise and concern. She did not tell Ari that these men were members of the Addicto gang and were friends of her brother, also a gang member.

Delia ordered a second glass of wine but declined dessert or coffee. Ari ordered coffee and apple pie.

Back at Delia's apartment, she invited him in. She poured a glass of wine for herself, lit a cigarette and said, "Can I get you something. It's unusual for a man not to drink."

"I still do some boxing, and I try to stay in training," he told her. He did not tell her of his promise to his mother.

They sat together on the couch. Ari smelled her perfume and, when she put her drink down, he put his arm around her, drew her to him and kissed her. She returned his kiss with ardor. After intense caresses led him to her bed.

The sex was the wildest and most passionate Ari had ever experienced. Afterwards they both lay exhausted and slept through the night. Ari woke in the morning, dressed, and left without disturbing her slumber.

He phoned her in the afternoon. "Last night was awesome," he told her. "Can I see you again? How about tonight?"

Delia agreed.

When Ari left work that afternoon he encountered three men, one of whom carried a shillelagh, the heavy Irish cane. It was obvious they intended to work him over.

The man with the cane never got to use it. Before he knew what was happening, Ari seized the cane and used it to flail the three, leaving them barely conscious and groaning on the sidewalk. He dropped the shillelagh on them and walked away, leaving a bystander to call for an ambulance.

In the evening after an exhausting repeat session in bed with Delia, she asked, "How come you're so damn strong?"

"It's my hair," he said. "As long as I don't cut it, I keep my strength." Delia relayed this information to her brother.

Ari now spent every night with Delia. Sometimes he took her out for dinner, and at other times they ordered pizza or Chinese, but the main event was their love making.

One evening Delia lit a joint. As she smoked she described the pleasurable effect of the marijuana to Ari. "It's great, and it's not like smoking tobacco." She pleaded with him to try it. Finally, Ari agreed, and they shared the joint. He liked the feeling it gave him, and thereafter they smoked together. Ari remembered the promise he made to his mother, but since it was not tobacco, he felt it did not matter. A few nights later, while sharing a joint after love making, Delia pressed him to try some wine. At this point, he neglected the promise, sampled the wine, and liking it, drank more.

The next day Delia phoned her brother again and made an arrangement. That evening Delia and Ari smoked several joints and finished most of a bottle of sacramental wine. When Ari lapsed into a deep sleep, Delia took scissors and cut off most of his hair. As arranged, her brother, together with other gang members, entered the apartment and injected Ari with crystal meth, a potent drug. When it was obvious he was incapable of resistance, they forced him into a car and drove him to their factory. They put drops of some chemical into his eyes and left him there.

When Ari awoke, he was almost completely blind and tied securely with rope. He recalled his mother's dying prediction—*If you smoke, drink, or use drugs, something bad will happen*—and something bad had happened. Ari tried to break free of the rope, but he could not. His strength was gone.

The Addicto gang members kept him in the factory day after day. They gave him barely enough food and water to keep him alive, and continued to drug him until he became an addict. He was blind and suffered the torments of craving the drug.

The lab for making crystal meth was in a dangerous place. Located in a wooden structure on the outskirts of the Bronx, it had once served as a warehouse. Unknown to the police, the entire gang of thirty-two lived there with their girlfriends in jerry-rigged apartments. Sleeping bags served as beds, and stoves, fired by propane or gasoline, were used for cooking. The building lacked running water and sanitary facilities

Ari was kept in the lab with one or more gang members to guard him, although his blindness prevented his escape. He slept on a bundle of old rags, and at night, was led outside to relieve himself. He was forced to carry out barrels of their trash and to sweep the lab after he had memorized the location of benches, chairs, and other structures. The gang used a metal ring around his neck, attached to a chain, to lead him around like a dog on a leash. The girls amused themselves by taking turns in leading him around as he performed his chores.

Ari's assistant at the pizzeria reported him missing, and the police searched for him in hospitals and flophouses to no avail. They concluded he had left town.

Months passed. Ari became filthy, unshaven, and his hair once again reached his shoulders. One Sunday morning, Ari awoke with a terrible craving. Some of the gang members were working at the benches making the drug. They laughed at Ari who pleaded for the drug and taunted him. "We'll give you a fix after you clean the place up," they told him. Ari sat on his rags in misery. His craving became rage. He realized he must finish this once and for all. He must pay for his transgressions.

Ari stood and made his way to the benches where two gang members were working. They tried to keep him away, but now his strength had returned. He pushed them both to the floor. With his arms he swept the tops of the benches where chemicals mixed, ignited and burst into flame. In minutes the lab was ablaze. Ari staggered to the doorway and stood there, preventing the panicked members from fleeing. He hurled them back into the burning lab. A tremendous explosion engulfed Ari and the gang members, turning them into human torches.

The blaze spread to the rest of the building, and in a short time, the entire structure was an inferno. No one got out. By the time the fire department arrived the warehouse was a furnace. They could only watch as it became completely consumed.

Ari's death had served a useful end. The entire Addicto gang and their factory were destroyed. For years to come, the neighborhood was freed of the drug makers.

THURSDAY NIGHTS AT BLOOMIES

It's not that I had never been shopping before, but following a divorce, I'd found myself involved in the intricacies of cooking, cleaning and doing laundry. At the supermarket, I had to choose cereals and detergents from a bewildering range of offerings and select produce that I could cook. Laundromats posed new problems. I recalled the dictum of separating the white from the colored. Watching my laundry go round and round in the washer, I fantasized about meeting a beautiful girl who was an accomplished laundress, a gourmet cook, and a nymphomaniac devoted only to me.

Despite these challenging homemaking activities, I was still left with boring evenings. Eventually, I thought of Bloomingdales on 59th and Lex. Thereafter, I spent every Thursday evening wandering through the aisles of that great emporium, seldom making a purchase, but perusing the offerings in Housewares, Men's Wear, and Linens.

I like good coffee as much as the next guy, and so an ad in the newspaper for a coffeemaker, whet my interest. Bloomingdales offered the Instabrewer for $29.95, purported to make super coffee. The ad called to mind an excellent cup of coffee I enjoyed years before at the old La Fonda Del Sol Restaurant in the Time-Life Building. The waiter prepared the coffee tableside, and when I complimented him on its flavor, he displayed the coffeemaker.

"It's called the French Press," he said with a Castilian accent. "Forty-four beans per cup."

The Instabrewer in the ad looked like the French Press. I decided I would go down to Bloomingdales that evening to investigate.

Arriving at the Housewares Department on The Sixth Floor, I showed the ad to one of the salesmen.

"Does it make good coffee?" I asked. Of course, I realized that the question was akin to asking a waiter if the fish was fresh.

"Oh, yes," he assured me.

"How does it work?" I inquired.

"It's easy," he told me. "You just put some ground coffee in it, pour in boiling water, wait 5 minutes and then push the plunger. The plunger has a filter, and you know, it pushes the grounds to the bottom. That's all there is to it."

"And the coffee is really good?" I persisted.

"Yeah."

A small group of shoppers had gathered around us, listening to our conversation with the innate curiosity typical of New Yorkers.

"How about making me a cup of coffee with it?" I asked.

The young man's eyes widened with shock. "I can't do that, sir. I'm—"

"Sure you can," I interrupted.

The Floor Manager, carnation in buttonhole, approached. "What seems to be the problem?" he inquired.

"This gentleman asked me to make him a cup of coffee with the Instabrewer," the salesman said.

As if I had asked him to cook a gourmet meal.

"I just want to try some coffee with the Instabrewer," I explained.

The manager smiled. "Of course. By all means." Turning to the salesperson, he ordered in an imperious manner, "Make this gentleman a cup of coffee." The manager nodded to me and the onlookers and strode away. Nearby, several salespeople pointed at me whispering "company rep."

As the salesperson scurried off, several of the shoppers asked me what was happening. I explained I was interested in the Instabrewer and wanted a demonstration.

"Does it make good coffee?" a man asked.

"Yes," I said with a conviction I had yet to feel. "It makes terrific coffee." I demonstrated how it worked.

"I think I want one, too," the man said.

"So do I," several of the women chorused.

I was amused by the situation. *What's going on here? I'm a college professor, not a salesman. But apparently I'm now selling Instabrewers.*

The salesman returned with an Instabrewer full of coffee and a cup. He filled the cup for me, apologizing for the lack of cream or sugar. I tasted the coffee, as a connoisseur would savor a vintage wine. I was tempted to extend my pinky. The group watched in expectation.

"Excellent," I declared. At least three of the group besieged the salesman with orders for Instabrewers. "Thanks for helping," he told me. I bought one, too.

Another Thursday found me back in Housewares seeking to buy an electric can opener. I waited patiently while the salesman, not the one who makes coffee, helped a customer select some wood stain. He produced a stained sample for her inspection.

"This is the walnut," he said.

The woman studied it for a moment. "It's nice," she said, "but . . ."

He showed her another sample. "And this is the oak, again."

I could see that he couldn't help adding the "again".

"That one's nice, too," she wavered.

What followed next were samples of chestnut, ebony, cherry, rosewood and maple.

The salesman sighed struggling to suppress exasperation. "These are all I have."

"I just don't know," she said.

This interchange continued for fifteen minutes. The woman picked up one of the samples, studied it, sighed, and put it down, as he waited. But I had grown impatient. I turned to the woman and asked, "What are you staining?"

"It's for my kitchen," she said.

"And what's your kitchen like?" I asked.

"It has this wooden part, sort of like a big board with copper pans hanging on it, and I want to stain it."

I had noticed some copper pots and pans displayed at a counter. I grabbed a number of stain samples, took her arm, and led her to the display of copper pans. I held up one of the stain samples near the pans, examined it, and then tried another. The woman watched me eagerly. When I tested the oak sample, I nodded sagely and pronounced in a judicial tone, "This is the one you want."

The woman seemed pleased with my decision and together we marched back to the salesman where she ordered a can of oak stain and departed.

This is absurd. Now I'm selling wood stain.

He thanked me. "That woman has been trying to get me to make up her mind for at least two weeks. She stops in, I show her the samples, and she leaves without buying anything. Thanks for helping."

My boring evenings came to a welcome end when the departmental chairman sent Jennifer, an attractive young graduate student, into my laboratory for training. It didn't take long for us to fall in love.

Christmas came around and one Thursday evening Jennifer suggested, "Let's go down to Bloomies. We can shop for each other's Christmas presents and then meet for dinner."

After half an hour, having considered a myriad of perfumes, baubles, bangles and beads, I made my way into the Lingerie Department. It was crowded, and I stood at a counter waiting to be helped. A young woman about ten feet away stood at the same counter. She was in her early thirties, pretty. She examined a counter-top rack displaying half a dozen pairs of panties. Small lacy things. I watched as she selected a white pair and held it up for a closer look. *She doesn't look like the type for white lingerie,* I mused. She turned her head towards me aware of my presence. In that instant, our eyes met, and I shook my head. She dropped the panties like a small child who had been caught touching a forbidden thing. She selected another, this time a black pair, held them up and looked at me, her eyes questioning. *Uh-uh, she's not the type for black either.* Again, I shook my head. Dropping the black ones, she now selected a pink pair and looked at me, obviously wanting my reaction. Neither of us smiled. This time I nodded approval. A salesgirl approached her, and the woman bought the pink pair. She walked away without another glance in my direction. I bought the black ones.

Some weeks later, Jennifer and I attended a cocktail party at the university to introduce a new faculty member to our department. Following a brief introduction by the department chair, Jennifer and I, drinks in hand, meandered through the small crowd making our way to the new addition. He was a good-looking young man, dressed in a navy blazer. An attractive young woman stood by his side, talking to another guest. I introduced

Jennifer and myself to him and we shook hands. “Welcome to our department,” I said. “We’re glad to have you. After you’re successful postdoc, what lead you to choose Columbia?” “Actually,” he said, “I had a good offer from UCLA too, but Victoria and I discussed it, and she persuaded me to come here.” His partner had finished her conversation and turned to face me and her eyes widened as her face paled in recognition. She was the young woman who bought the pink panties! Her young man saw her reaction. “Do you two know each other?” I smiled and said, “No, I’m sure we’ve never meet. I would never forget such a charming lady”, I added. I sensed her relief as Victoria composed herself and said, “I guess I helped to persuade Donald to come here.”

“Everyone needs a little help once in a while,” I said.

SINGULARITY

Benjamin Ross left his home at ten o'clock in the evening and drove for an hour and a half until he reached the desert. He found the dirt road and followed it for another thirty minutes until it came to an end. He killed the engine, ate one of the two sandwiches his wife had prepared, and drank some of the coffee from the thermos, still scalding hot. He settled down preparing to wait until morning.

As the hours passed, it got colder in the car. Unable to sleep, Benjamin had to run the engine from time to time so the heater could provide warmth.

When the first streaks of light appeared, Benjamin ate the other sandwich, finished the coffee, and got out of the car. He retrieved his carbine, a Winchester Model 94 lever-action 30-30. He took three cartridges from a small box, stuffing the box back into his pocket. Benjamin fed the rounds into the magazine, levered one into the chamber, and set the hammer at the safe, half-cocked position.

Benjamin started out heading west, and when the sky began to redden he declared, "Hail Aurora, thou rosy-fingered goddess of the dawn." Then he laughed. Benjamin did not believe in gods or goddesses.

He continued to walk, startled when a large jack rabbit bolted from a clump of brush, running with large leaps like a small kangaroo. Benjamin threw the carbine to his shoulder and followed the bounding rabbit but did not fire. He hoped to get a deer.

After an hour of walking, he came to the edge of a large canyon. Peering down, he thought he saw movement. Yes! It was a mule deer that disappeared into the bottom of the canyon.

Benjamin started down a steep narrow trail. He realized if he shot the deer he would never be able to pack it out of the canyon, but he continued. Without warning, he lost his footing, slipped on loose stones, and tumbled headfirst downwards. His head struck a large rock, and he lost consciousness.

Benjamin woke in pain. He laid on his back on a sort of mat. His head throbbed, and when he reached his hand up to touch it, he encountered a bandage or poultice. His hip and knee were painful. It was dark, and he seemed to be in an enclosure, a cave or hut. Benjamin tried to get up but only succeeded in groaning. A man appeared looking down at him.

The man spoke, "Don't try to get up." The man knelt and proffered a small wooden cup. "Drink this." He supported Benjamin's head so he could drink. It was a broth of some kind, warm, and salty. "Now sleep," the man said, and Benjamin slept.

The next time Benjamin awoke the man stood beside him. He looked to be about forty, with long white hair secured by a ribbon around his forehead to keep the hair out of his eyes. His face was tanned with blue eyes, a white handlebar moustache, and a white neatly cropped beard. The man wore sandals and was dressed in a tunic, which left his arms bare and reached down to his knees. It looked as if it was made of animal skins. "Thank you for helping me," Benjamin said. "May I ask your name?"

The man smiled. "You can call me Gus."

"Where am I?" Benjamin asked.

"You are in my hut."

"How did I get here?"

"I carried you down from where you fell."

"Should I be in a hospital?"

"You have no broken bones," Gus told him. "You will mend here." Benjamin wondered how Gus could make this assertion without X-rays, but decided not to push the point.

"Are you hungry?" Gus asked.

"Yes, I could eat something."

Gus turned and walked to the rear of the hut and returned with a wooden bowl, which he handed to Benjamin. On inspection, the bowl contained small pieces of meat together with what looked like rice, a vegetable and a fork. The food was warm. Benjamin could not identify the meat, but it tasted good, and he finished everything. Gus watched while he ate. Taking the empty bowl from Benjamin to the back of the hut, he returned with a wooden cup.

"Drink this," Gus told him. "It will help you to mend and to sleep." Benjamin drank the liquid, began to feel sleepy, lay back and was soon asleep again.

Days passed during which Benjamin was soon able to sit. Gus changed the dressing on his head everyday.

"How long have you lived here, Gus?"

"I have always lived here," Gus said. Gus did not talk much, he answered Benjamin's questions but was otherwise silent. Benjamin's strength gradually returned. He was able to stand although he still felt weak. He explored the back of the hut and found a small fireplace of stones. There was no other bed. *Where did Gus sleep*, he wondered? Benjamin's carbine stood in the corner.

More days passed. Benjamin was able to walk out of the hut and sit on a large rock near the doorway. Sometimes Gus would leave, walk down along the canyon floor, and disappear for an hour or so, always returning. Benjamin wondered whether police were searching for him. Alice, his wife, would surely have called 911 when he failed to return home.

"Have there been people looking for me?" he asked Gus one day.

Gus simply smiled and said, "No, no one has been looking for you, but you are ready to return to your home."

Benjamin was elated. He dusted off his clothes. His jeans were torn. He walked into the hut and retrieved his carbine. He worked the lever, ejecting three cartridges. Picking them up, he was startled to see they appeared different from the 30-30 rounds he had always used. He retrieved the cartridge box from his pocket and saw the three cartridges were identical to the others in the box. He examined the box, which read 38-55 caliber. He examined the carbine. On the side was etched, Winchester Model 94 cal 38-55.

He turned to Gus. "This is not my rifle," he said.

"Surely, it is," Gus told him. "It was next to you when I found you. There is no other rifle here."

Benjamin reached for his wallet. "I want to pay you," he said, only to find his wallet missing. Gus walked into the hut and returned with the wallet, which he handed to Benjamin. "You can not pay me," he said with a smile. Benjamin took the wallet. It appeared untouched.

Gus accompanied Benjamin up the trail leading out of the canyon. They reached the top after an hour's climb. Gus pointed in the direction Benjamin should walk. "You will find your vehicle there," he said before he turned, and without another word, started back down the path.

Benjamin found his car, which to his surprise, started immediately. He turned around, found the dirt road, then the highway, and eventually reached his home. To his surprise his house was now surrounded by a low white picket fence. He checked the house number and the street to assure himself it was his house. He went in to be greeted by Alice. "Oh, you've hurt yourself, and your jeans are torn. Are you okay?"

"That's all you have to say?" Benjamin asked. "I must have been gone for weeks!"

Alice laughed, "What are you talking about? You left here last night."

"When did you have the fence installed?" he asked.

"Are you kidding? You put the fence up yourself two years ago," she said and looked at him quizzically. "Go and wash up, dinner is ready."

Later, at the table with Alice, their kids joined them, together with a black Labrador Retriever.

"Hi Dad," Ted, his 13 year old, greeted him followed by 10 year old Andrea, who kissed him, before they both sat.

"What dog is that?" Benjamin asked.

"It's Sheba," Andrea told him. The dog ran over to Benjamin wagging her tail and licking his hand. Benjamin was confused. The Sheba he knew was yellow, but he did not say anything. He noticed his son was wearing a new wristwatch.

"That's a fine looking watch," he told Ted. "Where did you get it?"

His son looked at him strangely. "You gave it to me last Christmas, Dad," the boy said. "Don't you remember?"

Later, in bed with Alice, he leaned over to kiss her goodnight. "I like your perfume. Is it new?"

Alice turned to him. "It's the same perfume I've worn for years. Are you all right, Benjamin?" she asked. Benjamin was not all right. Something was wrong, but he did not know what.

The next day was Monday, and he went to his office. His secretary and co-workers greeted him and everything seemed okay until he observed his computer, a Dell when he left last week, was now a Hewlett Packard, but he found all his programs were the same.

The following Saturday, Benjamin was determined to go back to the canyon. Somehow he felt Gus would be able to explain what had happened. He told Alice he would return in a few hours. He drove back to the desert, found the dirt road, and walked to the canyon. He picked his way down the trail taking care not to fall again. When he reached the bottom he looked around. There was no hut. There was no sign there ever had been a hut, although he was able to identify the large rock that had been just outside the hut's door.

Benjamin sat down on the rock and tried to figure out what had happened. He called to mind the change in his carbine, the picket fence, Sheba's color, his son's wristwatch, Alice's perfume and his changed computer. What did it mean? He sat there for hours but could not think of a rational explanation. It must be me. Maybe I have had some kind of a stroke or something.

Dejectedly, he started back up the trail, found his car and drove home. The picket fence was still there and everything was the same. After dinner he called to his new Sheba. "C'mon old girl. Let's go for a walk." He attached her leash and started, heading down the block the way he always had before. It was dark and as he approached the corner, he observed a fire hydrant that he had never seen. In exasperation, he looked up at the sky. Benjamin saw two moons shining in the night sky.

THE MAN WHO LOST HIS SHADOW

Until three days ago when the phenomenon, or whatever it was, occurred, Irving Loren had been a contented man. But then it happened, and he could not, for the life of him, explain it. It was disturbing.

He and Cynthia lived in a modest house in Norwalk, Connecticut, close to the beach. Their two children now grown and married had kids of their own. Since his retirement three years ago, Irving spent much of his waking hours reading and taking walks on the beach with Cynthia.

"Let's take a walk, Irv," Cynthia said. It was a beautiful sunny Saturday morning, the Fourth of July, with the promise of beach parties and fireworks. He grabbed a baseball cap, and together they walked to the beach. The sun shone in his eyes, and he pulled the visor lower. They strolled on the hard packed sand along the water's edge. The tide was out, and the air had the fresh fishy smell of things the sea leaves when it recedes. They chatted about the children and the grandchildren. After thirty minutes they turned to go back. As they walked along, he glanced down at the sand. There was Cynthia's shadow, dark and clearly defined, but he did not have one. That's curious, Irving thought. Some trick of the light? Maybe I was behind her.

Irving moved around to walk beside her, still no shadow. He picked up his pace, anxious to get back to the house before Cynthia could notice the aberration.

"Would you like a glass of lemonade, Hon?" Cynthia asked. Irving nodded, still pondering the absence of his shadow as he gulped the cool drink.

Irving had been a high school science teacher for forty years with a good grasp of basic physics. He knew visible light simply does not pass through a solid body, but produces a shadow. But where is mine? What could explain it?

Irving recalled the Dracula movies of years ago where the vampire, Bela Lugosi, did not have a reflection in the mirror. He finished his lemonade and walked to the mirror in the front hall trying to appear inconspicuous. He was relieved to see the same aging face and graying hair he saw every morning when he shaved. Irving felt ridiculous.

That night as he lay in bed next to his wife, Irving continued to wonder about the loss of his shadow. Cynthia had been reading, her book had fallen to her chest, and she snored lightly. He got up, put her book away, kissed her gently on the forehead and turned off her bedside lamp. How can a man's shadow just disappear? How long has my shadow been gone?

Sunday it rained, and Irving felt frustrated. He was anxious to see if it had really happened. Maybe I just imagined it?

Monday morning was bright and sunny. Cynthia was in the kitchen preparing a casserole for dinner.

"I'm going for a walk," Irving called to her, grabbed his cap and set off for the beach before she could offer to come with him. The tide was low, and he walked into the sun, not yet willing to look and see if his shadow was there. A large rock, not far off shore, caught his attention. As Irving drew closer, he could see a young woman sunning herself on it. He was surprised to see she was nude—at least the upper half of her body was nude, the lower half was in the water. Her straight hair was the color of jade, and hung to her shoulders. Irving had never seen green hair. She was pretty with small breasts. He walked towards her wanting to get a better look.

"Hi," he called, curious to learn more about this strange young woman.

She smiled at him and said, "Hello."

Irving noticed a couple walking towards them along the previously deserted beach. "Some people are coming, and they'll see you," he warned.

"They can't see me," she said.

"Why not? I can see you."

"They can't."

Irving realized her mouth didn't move as she spoke to him. Her words just came into his head. Her voice sounded like the ringing of a bell. She had an enchanting smile.

"So how come I can see you and they can't?" he asked. Irving wondered whether it had something to do with his lack of a shadow. She seemed to read his mind.

"You've become like one of us, the Sea People. We have no souls, you know," she said.

"What's your name?" he asked for want of something else to say.

"I'm called Meara. What are you called?"

"Irving."

The couple had now walked past where he stood and did not appear to notice anything unusual. Irving hoped that they did not see him talking to an empty ocean.

"Would you like to come and live with me, Irving?" Meara asked.

"I would miss my wife," he said, "but maybe I could come for a visit."

"No," she said. "You couldn't do that. Once you come to the sea you can never return to the land."

"Anyway, you're too young for me," Irving told her. She looked to be about twenty-five.

Meara laughed, a tinkling in his head, "I'm a hundred and twelve and have many children. They're all gone now, and I'm lonely. I have to go. Goodbye, Irving," she said sadly. She turned and dove into the water with a splash. He saw the lower half of her body resembled a great fish.

Irving turned his back to the sun and started for home. There was no shadow. In desperation, he walked over to a vacant lifeguard tower. The tower cast a strong shadow, but no matter how he positioned himself next to it, he had none. Have I lost my soul? Is that what's happened to me?

Irving became despondent, lost his appetite, and moped around the house. He found excuses not to go outside during the day and grew pale. At night he dreamed of swimming deep in a cerulean sea following Meara, her green hair streaming behind her.

"You don't look well, Irv," Cynthia said. "Are you sick?"

"I'm okay," he told her. But I am sick, he realized. I must have some kind of a mental illness. I have no shadow, maybe no soul, and I've talked to a mermaid. I need help. I can't go on like this.

Irving found a psychiatrist, a Doctor Myron Wexler, and arranged for an evening appointment.

"What led you to come to see me?" Dr. Wexler asked.

Irving looked around as if to make certain they were alone.

"I have lost my shadow," he whispered.

"What?" the doctor asked.

"I have hallucinations—things which aren't possible. It's driving me crazy. I have no shadow, and I've seen a mermaid. Talked with her, dreamed about her! Can you help me?"

"Do you drink alcohol?" the doctor asked.

"Just a glass of wine now and then with dinner."

"Do you use recreational drugs?"

Irving shook his head.

"Have you recently had any kind of head injury, a fall perhaps?"

"No."

"To begin with, we can start you on medication," Dr. Wexler said.

"What kind of medication?"

"One of the anti-psychotic drugs."

"Am I psychotic?" Irving asked.

"I don't think so, but I would need to do some tests," Dr. Wexler said.

"The medicine might help."

Irving felt medicine would not solve his problem.

"No, I don't want any pills," Irving told him. "Thanks anyway."

Two weeks passed. Cynthia seemed concerned about his apathy. "How about a movie tonight?" she asked. "We can go after dinner. *The Wild Ones* is playing at the Apollo."

Irving watched the movie without much interest until the film depicted a group of high school students on a beach sitting around a bonfire. As he sat in the dark theater, a different scene in his mind replaced the one on the screen. Irving recalled another Fourth of July, thirty-eight years ago. He remembered it vividly. It had been a hot and humid day. Cynthia and the kids were in Ohio visiting her mother, and he had become bored and lonely. He missed Cynthia. Toward evening he had a few drinks and decided to go for a swim. He pulled on bathing trunks and walked to the beach.

A large group of young people was gathered around a bonfire. Someone played a guitar, and Irving could smell the scent of marijuana. He stood and watched them. A girl detached herself from the group and approached him.

"Hi, Mr. Loren," she said with a smile. "Nice to see you again."

Irving recognized Jill Fowler, one of his former students. Her class had graduated just a month ago. Jill had been one of the brightest students in his science class and the prettiest. She was as tall as he with a slim feminine figure barely covered by a bikini.

"Wanna take me for a walk?" she asked in a provocative tone.

"Sure". Her directness was different from the Jill he knew.

Jill linked her arm through his and steered him away from the fire. They walked along the water's edge letting the dying waves wash over their bare feet. She held his arm against her body so he could feel her firm young breast. He was surprised at this intimacy but did not pull away from her. They continued along for about fifteen minutes and were soon out of sight of the group. Irving looked at the calm water and thought of swimming. It would be fun to swim naked—no one was around to see. Irving remembered his high school days when friends bragged about skinny-dipping with girls. He had never done it. Why not now?

On a wild impulse, Irving said huskily, "Wanna go skinny-dipping?" Jill giggled and stripped off her bikini. There was no moon, but fireworks from across the harbor began to appear in the sky and in their light he could see her form, an enticing nymph.

"C'mon," she called and raced into the water. Irving pulled off his trunks and followed her. The water was cool and refreshing. He heard her splashing ahead of him and swam out to her. The tide was going out, drawing them further from the beach. They swam and splashed about for a few minutes. Irving was excited to be swimming naked with this beautiful young girl. He resisted the urge to touch her.

The swim back to the beach against the tide had tired them and they fell on the warm sand close to each other. They lay on their backs, out of breath, gazing at the stars. Jill rested her head on his out-stretched arm. Irving drew her close to him and kissed her.

"Mmm," she whispered, "that was nice. What about your wife,

Mr. Loren?"

"My wife is in Ohio, and what she doesn't know won't hurt her."

He tried to explore her body with his sandy hand.

"Hey, that feels rough," she protested.

Irving bent and kissed one breast. He felt her nipple harden in his mouth.

"Oh," Jill gasped. She pushed him down and kneeled over him, taking him into her mouth.

Irving felt like he was in a dream. Jill shifted to envelop his tumescence and began to move. She was tight, wet, and hot. Irving moaned with pleasure. A star shell exploded overhead, punctuating their climax. Jill collapsed and lay on him.

"That was awesome, Mr. Loren," she panted.

The sex had been fast, but great. Better than anything Irving could remember. This was the first time since his marriage to Cynthia he had had sex with another woman.

Jill rolled away to lie at his side. After a few minutes, she said, "I'm coming down. I need another toke. Let's go back."

They put on their swimsuits over sandy bodies and started back. As they walked along, holding hands, Irving could not wait to get away from her. He wished it hadn't happened.

When they came within sight of the group around the fire,

Irving said, "I don't know what came over me."

Jill giggled. "Forget it, Mr. Loren. It was like—fantastic. G'night."

Irving slunk home, showered and got into bed, but he could not sleep. What have I done? I committed adultery, and I had sex with a student. Well, a former student. It's twice as bad—unforgivable. He could never tell Cynthia, it would hurt her. Would she ever forgive him? There was no excuse, but he would never do it again.

Cynthia and the kids returned home the next day. Irving tried, without success, to push the previous night's escapade from his mind, but the vision of Jill above him on the sand kept recurring. As the years went by, he would occasionally recall the episode, but he returned it to the oblivion of his memory.

Now, thirty-eight years later, Irving sat in the movie theater next to Cynthia. He was covered with sweat, waiting impatiently for the movie to end. He recognized how he had lost his soul and his shadow.

Irving watched a lot of TV during the day. On one sit-com, he saw a priest comfort a young woman who was depressed. Maybe a priest could help me?

Irving found Father O'Neill in a church in Westport. The priest was in his forties and wore a black cassock with a Roman collar. He greeted Irving with a smile.

"I need help, Father. Can you help me?"

The priest led him into the sacristy.

"How can I help you, Mr.—?"

"Loren, Irving Loren. Is what I tell you kept secret?" Irving asked.

"Yes. Anything told to a clergyman or a doctor is privileged communication. Even in a court of law."

"If I tell you about something I did—something bad—a long time ago, can you—you know—make it okay?"

"Are you Catholic, Mr.—?"

"Loren. No, I'm Jewish."

"I'm sorry Mr. Loren, but confession and absolution are only for

Catholics. Perhaps you might talk to a rabbi."

More weeks went by. Irving was in torment. On a Friday evening he sought out the rabbi at a local synagogue. He waited around until the service was over and the congregants had left.

"Can I talk with you a minute, Rabbi?" Irving asked.

Rabbi Seligman looked to be about Irving's age. He smiled and offered his hand. "Certainly. I don't believe we've met Mr.—?"

"Loren, Irving Loren."

The rabbi ushered Irving into his office with a desk and two comfortable chairs. They each sat.

"I'm not a member here," Irving started.

"We'd be happy to welcome you," Rabbi Seligman said, "but how can I help you?"

"Is it—you know, confidential—privileged?"

Rabbi Seligman smiled. "Sure, what's the problem?"

"I did something bad many years ago, and now it's making me ill. It's like a big piece of meat stuck in my throat. I'm unable to cough it up, and I can't swallow it."

The rabbi nodded, "A sin."

"Can you absolve me from it? I could tell you about it, if I have to."

"We don't believe in that sort of thing," the rabbi said. "Only God can forgive sins against Him. In sins where you have injured someone, only that person can forgive."

Now Irving knew what his sin was and what he had to do. He had to find Jill and ask for her forgiveness.

Irving phoned the high school and tried to find out where Jill had gone after graduation.

"You say she was in the Class of 1968? That's a long time ago. Those records must be in the basement," the clerk told him. "I'll try to find them. Could you call back in a day or so?"

Irving waited two days and then called the clerk again.

"I've got bad news, Mr. Loren. Our basement was flooded some years ago and those records were destroyed. I'm sorry," she said.

Irving looked in the local phone book. Perhaps he could find her parents if they were still alive, but the three Fowlers he was able to locate told him they had no daughters. Irving became more depressed.

He tried the local newspaper. They usually listed the names in each graduating class. After two days of searching microfiche files in a dusty basement, he found her. Jill had planned to attend the University of Connecticut in Storrs. He phoned the University and asked for information about the Class of 1972. This time the clerk was more helpful.

"Yes, Miss Fowler was in the Nursing Program. When she graduated, she started to work at the Hartford Hospital."

"What's with all these telephone calls?" Cynthia asked.

"I'm trying to find someone I knew many years ago," he told her. "It's important." Cynthia shrugged.

Irving phoned the Human Resources Department at the Hartford Hospital. "We have no record of a Jill Fowler working here," he was told. In desperation, Irving drove to Storrs. At the University Library he found the Alumni Directory for the Class of 1972. There she was! She had married a doctor, Glen Burton, and they were living in Farmington. There was an address and phone number.

Irving left the library and used his cell phone. With trembling hands, he dialed the number. Please, please let her be there.

"Hello?"

"I'd like to speak to Jill Fowl—Burton."

"This is Jill Burton. Who's calling?"

"It's Irving Loren," he said huskily. "Your old high school teacher."

"Mr. Loren." Her voice was enthusiastic. "How nice to hear from you. How are you?"

"I'm fine. Jill, can I come over to see you? I need to talk to you."

"You mean now, this afternoon?"

"Yes, if it's convenient."

Irving followed her directions and reached her large house in a suburban community. It had a well-manicured lawn with flowering shrubs near the house.

Jill greeted him warmly. "This is a surprise, Mr. Loren. How nice to see you." Jill had aged gracefully and was now a handsome woman. Her face was still pretty though her hair showed a few strands of grey. He followed her into a well-appointed living room where they sat. "Can I offer you something to drink? Some coffee?"

Irving shook his head. "How have you been, Jill?" he asked.

"Just fine. I'm a nurse, and my husband is a surgeon at the Hartford Hospital. We have two grown children. I'm curious, what led you to come to see me?"

"Do you remember that night—the Fourth of July, on the beach?"

Her face colored. "Yes," she said. "I do." Her voice took on a serious tone. "As I recall, we—you know."

"Jill—don't know how to say this, but—you know what happened . . . "

She looked at him questioningly. "Yeah—it was a wild night."

"We—I shouldn't have—well, taken advantage of you," Irving said.

"As I remember, Mr. Loren, I sort of led you on."

"Anyway, I'm sorry," Irving said.

Jill looked confused. "That was—let me see—about forty years ago. Why bring it up now? What are you sorry about?"

"I can't explain. I just need—I'm sorry to have hurt you."

"Look, Mr. Loren, I was stoned, and maybe you had a few drinks. It shouldn't have happened, but it did. So what?"

"I'd like to do something to—well, make it right," Irving persisted. "Is there anything I can do?"

Jill laughed. "Sure, you can pay off the mortgage."

"I'm serious, Jill," he said, tears coming to his eyes. "I need you to forgive me."

"Why? I wasn't hurt, and I hope you weren't. There is nothing to forgive. I don't understand why this matters after all these years."

"Could you—I mean, just say it—just say 'I forgive you'?" he pleaded.

Jill regarded him with compassion. Her tone softened, and in a low voice, she said, "Okay, Mr. Loren, I forgive you."

At the door, Jill kissed him on the cheek. "Take care of yourself, Mr. Loren," she said.

It was dark when Irving reached home. Cynthia had dinner waiting. "Where have you been all day?" she asked.

"I took a long drive and wound up in Farmington." Irving couldn't wait until the next day. He hoped his trial was over. He awoke early. The sun was already up.

"Let's take a walk," he said, trying not to show his anxiety. He and Cynthia started for the beach. The sun shone in their faces, but Irving did not look behind. The tide was coming in, and the air had a fresh, salty tang. Screeching gulls flew above the waves, and a squadron of sandpipers ran before them as if leading the way. They walked in silence until Irving felt he was ready. He took a deep breath, closed his eyes and said, "Okay, let's go back." They turned around and Irving opened his eyes. Only Cynthia's shadow was there. He was crushed. I guess it's too late. My soul is lost. Irving felt he was going to die.

Irving wanted to pray, but could not remember any prayers. A fragment came into his head. *The Lord is My Shepherd, I shall not want . . . He restoreth my soul.* Irving looked down at the sand ahead of him. Wait! Something was happening. Faint at first, but gradually it became darker and within another moment, his shadow was as dark as hers. Irving breathed a deep sigh. Cynthia looked at him and smiled. It was a smile of understanding. He took her hand and held it tightly.

"Yes," she said, "let's go home."

LITTLE PEOPLE

Up the airy mountain
Down the rushy glen
We daren't go a-hunting
For fear of little men...
The Fairies
William Allingham, 1854

Robin awoke to an unusual sound. She lay on her side in her sleeping bag, waiting to see if the sound would repeat. Was it a dream, she wondered? No, there it was again—a moan but high-pitched, as if from a child. Robin rolled over and reached across the floor of the hut to where her partner lay snoring in his sleeping bag.

"Wake up, Smitty," she whispered.

After a moment, he turned towards her and asked, "What's the matter, Robin? Are you okay?"

"Shush," she said in the dark hut. "I heard something."

Martin retrieved a flashlight and peered into the surrounding jungle. "Be careful, Martin," Robin whispered, as her colleague disappeared into the darkness.

The Indonesian jungle was rife with wildlife, including wild chickens, civet cats, monkeys, a deer-like pig, large fruit eating bats called "flying foxes", and dwarf buffalos. The most dangerous was the Komodo Dragon, huge predatory carnivorous lizards, who could run for short distances to catch their prey including humans.

Moments later, she heard him call, "Hey Robin, come look at this."

She stepped out of the hut to find Martin crouching over something on the ground. As she grew nearer, she was astounded to see what the flashlight illuminated—a humanoid creature, less than three feet tall, whose eyes stared up at the light with fear. It emitted pitiful cries and moans.

Robin Miller and Martin Smith were anthropologists. Robin was a professor at the University of Arizona and the senior member of the team, while Martin, an associate professor in the same department, was her colleague for many years. They were exploring on Flores, a remote island in the Indonesian Archipelago, searching for unique fossils.

Six years earlier, a team of Australian geologists working on Flores, astounded the scientific community by finding the skeletal remains of a woman who had been only three feet tall. They were working in a cave called Liang Bua. The bones, 18,000 years old, were originally thought to be those of a child, but later measurements confirmed the bones were those of a pre-modern adult woman. Nearby, the geologists found stone tools, spear points, and fireplaces. Bones of extinct pygmy elephants were also present showing evidence of butchering. The Australians reasoned that over the centuries, the elephants and the people gradually became small because of the limited food supply on the isolated island.

Robin and Martin were seeking additional sites of the Hobbit-sized beings. They were amazed when elders of the local Ngada tribe who lived at the base of an active volcano, recounted their ancestors traded with these "little people."

The Chief of the tribe told them a bizarre story. He related some of the tribesman captured a tiny woman about three weeks ago. She had come down from a cave on the volcano. She was about three feet tall. The Chief had not seen her himself because she managed to escape and disappear. The Chief said she could have been one of the Ebu Gogo, tiny hairy people who lived in the region long ago. The anthropologists were inclined to disbelieve the Chief's story.

"Maybe the creature was just a woman from a neighboring tribe who suffered from dwarfism or a similar disease," Martin suggested.

Now, in the pitch-blackness near the Liang Bua Cave, the two anthropologists stared down at the strange creature.

"Let's bring him into the hut," Martin said. "Careful, he may be hurt."

Together they carried the small being into the hut and laid him on the floor. After lighting their kerosene lamp, they turned to inspect him. It was immediately apparent the creature was female. She was thin, with olive colored skin, pendulous breasts, and a protruding belly. Hair covered her long arms, legs, and lower abdomen. Her head was small with a forehead sloping to her eyebrows. The only clothing she wore was a miniscule apron-like garment of leaves and palm fronds woven together barely covering her private parts.

"Don't be afraid," Robin said. "We won't hurt you." She gently stroked the tiny woman's head and smiled at her reassuringly.

Robin turned to Martin, "Do you realize what we have here? She's one of those Ebu Gogo's—alive! And we thought they were extinct."

Martin nodded. "We've got to try and help her." He began a careful examination, moving her limbs. As he moved her left leg, the tiny woman emitted a loud cry. Martin could feel the problem.

"Her leg is broken, either the tibia, or fibula, maybe both. We need to splint it. Let's just try to keep her quiet until daylight when I can go out and find something I can use for a splint. In the meantime, let's try and give her some Tylenol for the pain."

Robin opened their first-aid kit and retrieved the pills.

"How are you going to get her to swallow them?" Martin asked.

"Watch," Robin told him. She poured some water into a cup, knelt by the small woman and held one of the tablets between her thumb and forefinger. The woman followed her movements. With exaggerated slowness, Robin opened her mouth, stuck out her tongue, placed the tablet on her tongue, closed her mouth and swallowed some water. The pint-sized woman watched Robin with interest. Robin retrieved another tablet, placed it in the woman's hand, and offered her the cup of water while smiling encouragement. The wee woman imitated Robin's gestures by sticking out her tongue, placing the tablet on it, closing her mouth and drinking some water. In this way, Robin got her to take two more Tylenols. Robin nodded her head in approval and lay down near the woman to wait for dawn.

At first light, Martin went out to find some sticks he could use for a splint. While he was gone, Robin activated an MRE, the military Meals Ready to Eat, they had brought for food. This one contained scrambled eggs and sausage, which she offered to the tiny woman. The woman ate a small portion with obvious enjoyment.

Martin soon returned with two straight branches he had trimmed. He used the Ace bandage from the first aid kit and was able to splint the small woman's leg. Using their digital camera, Martin took some photos of the woman. She winced after each flash. Robin gave her two more Tylenols while Martin examined the leg.

"It's quite swollen," he said. "I'll have to go down to Ende, to get some help. The bone or bones need to be set. It'll take me most of today to get there so I'll be back sometime tomorrow. Will you be okay?"

"Of course," Robin said. "We'll be fine here in the hut. We have food and water."

After Martin left, Robin tried to make the small woman more comfortable. She knelt near her, smiled and said, "I don't know your language, but I wish we could talk. There's so much I want to ask you."

The tiny woman seemed to understand. She reached up and gently pulled Robin's head down towards her face. Robin resisted for a moment, but then acquiesced until their foreheads touched. Robin heard a voice in her head although the woman had not spoken.

"This is the way we can talk. My name is Wani. Thank you for caring for me."

Robin was so startled she sat bolt upright. "How—could you—can we . . ."

The woman shook her head and smiled, gesturing for Robin to renew the contact with their foreheads.

"This is the only way we can talk. How are you called?"

"I'm called Robin. But how are you able to talk like this?"

"My people have always been able to do it. We don't even have to touch heads if we are close."

"Are you in pain?" Robin asked.

"No, the white medicines helped."

Robin's back tired of bending over the woman. She helped her to a sitting position, propping her up on a backpack. Robin now sat on the floor next to the woman so she could maintain the head-to-head contact.

"How old are you, Wani?" Robin asked.

"I have lived one hundred and twelve of your years." She seemed to sense Robin's skepticism. "Yes, we live longer than the big people. Many of us live for one hundred and fifty years or more."

"Do you have any children?"

"These breasts have nourished five children—three sons and two daughters. My youngest son was killed when our fiery mountain erupted."

"I'm sorry," Robin told her. "Where do your people live?"

"We live in caves beneath the ground up on the fiery mountain."

"Are you married—do you have a husband—a man?"

"My mate was killed six of your years ago. He was caught and eaten by one of the dragons."

"I'm sorry," Robin said. "How many of your people are there? And why do you live on the mountain?"

"We grow fewer with each generation. We live in the caves to hide from the big ones. Many years ago, my grandfather told me, we used to live near the big ones and trade with them, but then they began to capture us and make us work for them as slaves, so we ran away to the mountain."

"How do you survive up there? What do you eat?"

"Our caves are safe and adequate. We live on fruit, herbs, and the eggs of the wild chickens. Sometimes we are able to kill a pig, but these we only cook at night so the smoke from our fire is not seen."

"Where did your people originate?"

"Our elders say we came from a place you call Africa, and together with the big ones we spread over the land called Europe. In ages past, we lived there in harmony with the big ones. They had many names for us. Here the big ones call us Ebu Gogo, but in Europe we were known as elves, gnomes, goblins, leprechauns, trolls, sprites, and hobbits."

These stories fascinated Robin. "What happened to cause your people to hide from—the big ones?"

"The big ones began to blame us for bad things which happened to them—a cow who stopped giving milk or a well that went dry. We were even accused of stealing their babies and substituting one of ours. They started to kill us. That is when we began to hide and live underground."

"That's too bad," Robin said. "How long will this hiding continue?"

"Our elders say the time of our race is almost over, and we will soon disappear from the earth."

The talks went on for many hours. From time to time, the little woman grew tired and needed to rest. Robin was intrigued and eager to learn more about Wani and her people. She imagined the excitement in the scientific community when she and Martin returned to America and released the story. It would be in every newspaper around the world!

Robin activated another MRE for lunch, which she shared with the woman. Afterwards, she expressed an interest in seeing the cave where the little people lived.

"I can take you and show you," the woman told her when their foreheads were touching again.

"How? You can't walk."

The woman smiled. "Help me to the door."

Robin helped the woman to stand on her good leg and hop to the door. The woman gave a strange sound, something like a low whistle. Within minutes, two more of the dwarf-sized people appeared. They were males, as evidenced by their bushy beards, trimmed to a few inches. They were shy.

"These are my sons," Wani explained to Robin.

The two little men spoke to Wani in a strange language that had many clicking sounds. After a minute or two, they disappeared into the jungle. They were back in half an hour with a litter constructed of boughs and branches.

The woman gestured for Robin to touch foreheads. "They will help me up the mountain. You can come if you will promise never to reveal our homes to other big ones." Robin nodded assent, and the two small men helped their mother to lie in the litter. They picked up the litter with ease, and together with Robin, started up the mountain. Robin tore a page from her notebook and scribbled a note to Martin. "Have gone with Wani, et al. Back soon. R." She tossed the note on his sleeping bag, took their camera, water, and a few MREs.

They walked for about forty minutes, stopping once or twice for a brief rest. The ascent grew steeper, and the ground rockier. The land became more open with occasional trees, brush and sparse vegetation. They finally stopped, as if they had arrived at their destination, but Robin could see nothing unusual. One of the sons pulled what appeared to be some fallen boughs and leaves aside to reveal the face of a huge rock. Robin could see a small hole not more than eighteen inches in diameter in the face of the rock. The two men appeared to dive into the hole, leaving Robin and Wani alone.

Robin took a few pictures of the hole. She touched foreheads with Wani.

"I wish I could go in," she said. Robin was far from obese, but there was no way her shoulders or hips could pass through the hole.

"You can come in," Wani told her, "if you want to, but it will take some time."

"What do I have to do?"

"We will help you." Wani peered into the cave and spoke a few words in their strange language. Then she sat down next to Robin and waited. After twenty minutes, one of her sons emerged carrying some kind of a gourd, containing a liquid.

"Drink this," Wani told her. "It will help."

Robin took the gourd and smelled it. The liquid was hot and had an odd, musty smell. I don't know what this is supposed to do, but I'll give it a try, she thought. She drank the entire amount, about a cup full. It tasted like mushroom soup. In a few minutes, everything became blurry, and Robin felt sleepy. She had a sensation of falling, but she was lying down and soon fell asleep.

When Martin returned to their hut the following day, he was surprised to find neither Robin nor the small woman were there. She had taken the camera, a canteen, and a few MREs. He did not see the note Robin had left. An errant breeze had blown it into the dark recesses of the hut. Had he read it Martin would still not have understood the references to Wani and the others. He stepped outside and began to call and shout her name.

Martin searched the area in vain for many hours until it became too dark to see. He wondered whether she may have fallen and was lying unconscious somewhere. He spent the night in the hut and started back to Ende the next day, planning to get a search party with dogs. It rained heavily that night.

When Robin awoke, her mouth felt dry. She was in total darkness. She had no idea where she was or how long she had been asleep. She tried to sit up but could not. Her shoulders and hips felt weak and painful. Then she remembered—that drink! What did it do to me?

As her eyes gradually became accustomed to the dimness, she could see she was in a large cave. A hole in the ceiling provided the only source of light. There appeared to be a fireplace in the center of the cave beneath the hole. There were several dark openings in the walls around the cave, but Robin could not see where they led. She seemed to be alone, but soon the two little men emerged from one of the openings, carrying Wani over to where Robin lay. The men set Wani next to Robin and disappeared back into one of the openings. Wani touched foreheads with her.

"How are you feeling?" the voice in her head asked.

"I feel dizzy," she replied.

"It will soon pass," Wani told her, "but you will be weak for some time. The potion we gave you loosened the muscles in your shoulders and hips so we could make you hug yourself and squeeze you into the cave. Would you like to eat now?"

Robin could discern small chairs, benches, and tables around the cave. More of the little people emerged and moved around in the cave. Robin remembered how Gulliver must have felt when he was captured by the Lilliputians.

Martin, together with a group of natives and a bloodhound, returned to the hut and searched the entire area, but the heavy rain had washed away any scent. He did not tell the natives about the Ebu Gogo. By day's end he was obliged to pack their gear and return to Ende. He telephoned the U.S. Consulate in Jakarta reporting Robin's disappearance and requested assistance. He was told they would contact the Indonesian military and try to have a helicopter search the area. He also notified the University of Arizona of Robin's disappearance. After several days of heavy rain, a helicopter flew over from Jakarta and searched the area for hours before returning to base.

Martin visited the Ngada village and tried to induce the Chief to search for Robin, but the Chief refused. He told Martin there were evil spirits in that area.

Martin returned to Ende and started home. He grieved for his lost colleague. She had been a good friend and a frequent guest in his home. He bemoaned the lack of evidence of their remarkable find. Robin had taken the camera with the photos, and there was only his story. He knew he would not be believed.

Robin became adjusted to her new surroundings. Life in the cave with Wani and the others proved to be interesting. She worried Martin would not know what happened to her and discussed this with Wani, but there was nothing that could be done. She had no writing materials to send a note to him. Robin decided she would spend a few months with Wani and her people before returning to civilization.

Another little woman brought food over to Robin and helped her to sit up and eat. "This is one of my daughter's," Wani told her. "She was captured by the big ones who took her down to their village. One of them even tried to mate with her, but she was able to escape and return home."

I guess the Chief's story about capturing one of the Ebu Gogos is true, Robin thought. "How old is your daughter?" Robin asked.

"She is sixty of your years."

About the same age as I am, Robin realized. The effect of the drug had gradually worn off. When it's time for me to go I'll just drink the stuff again and squirm out, Robin decided. She told Wani of her plan.

Wani shook her head. "No, my daughter, you cannot do that. That drug can only be used one time. To use it again is certain death."

SOMETIMES YOU JUST CAN'T WIN

Doug Houser walked out on the tarmac to his airplane, a Cessna 210 *Centurion*. It was a high-wing aircraft, with retractable gear, and seats for five passengers. He performed the careful preflight, got in, and started the engine. He set the altimeter, gyro compass, the transponder code, set the trim for takeoff, and opened the cowl flaps. He turned on the radio to Ground Control.

"Cessna 81650 ready to taxi."

"Standby for your flight plan. Here it comes." The plan was pretty much the same as the on he filed. He was headed for Washington D.C. He repeated the instructions on the radio.

"650 clear to taxi. Position and hold." On the runway, he switched to the tower frequency, holding the breaks and waiting. An aircraft flew over, landed, and eventually cleared the runway.

"Cessna 81650 cleared for takeoff."

"Roger," he replied, releasing the breaks and moving the throttle to full. The weather was perfect, ceiling and visibility unlimited. Even though the weather was ideal, Doug had opted to file an instrument flight plan, knowing that Washington was a busy place.

After a minute or so, the tower told him to contact a controller and wished him a pleasant flight. He changed frequencies and announced, "Cessna 81650 climbing to 6,000."

"Roger 650."

At 6,000 feet Doug leveled off and reduced power and fuel to cruise settings. He settled back for a pleasant flight.

Doug's first experience with flight occurred in WWII in the U.S. Navy. He specialized in aviation ordinance, declining training as an aerial gunner, in the hopes of surviving the war for better things. He was assigned to a headquarters squadron at a naval air station near Norfolk, Virginia. The squadron flew the SBD dive-bomber. It was tasked with monitoring the sea for German submarines, in an area a hundred miles north and south of the air station. The subs had been cleared from the area the previous year, and so the squadron's reconnaissance flights were all joyrides. Doug's job was to load the machine guns for the rear cockpit, check the other machine guns, and load the five hundred pound single bomb in the bomb bay. After each flight, he had to unload the machine guns and the bomb, check them for operation, and return them the gun locker and the magazine. On rare occasions when the aerial gunner for a flight was not available, Doug was offered the opportunity to take his place in the rear cockpit. The flights were long and boring, and sometimes the pilot showed Doug how to make climbs, descents, and turns. Doug loved it. After the war, Doug returned to college, and to medical school, and entered his career in academic medicine. He took flying lessons, qualifying as a Private Pilot, later with commercial and instrument ratings. As the years went by, he joined flying clubs, renting and aircraft whenever he and it were available, and his budget permitted. After many more years, now a professor at a prominent medical school, he and two other men joined to purchase the Cessna. One of the men was Charlie Houser, Doug's younger brother, who had flown bombers for the U.S. Air Force. The other owner was a friendly gynecologist. Go figure.

As the flight continued, Doug was transferred from one controller to another as he progressed. Near Washington, he was told to contact Washington Approach Control.

"Cessna 81650 with you at 6,000," he said.

"Roger 650, squawk 2744 and start descent to 2,000. Your traffic is a 727 at twelve o'clock."

"I've got him," Doug said, putting the new code in the transponder.

"Just follow him."

After a few minutes, Doug was told to contact the tower. He changed frequencies and was cleared to land. After he cleared the runway, he contacted Ground Control for taxi instructions to a Flight Service Station.

"After you get your airplane put away, give us a call," the ground controller said.

That's odd, Doug thought. He walked over to a phone at the FSS, and called Ground Control.

"Are you the pilot of Cessna 81650?"

"Yes, I am. What's the problem?"

"You violated P32."

"What's that?" Doug asked.

"That's the White House. You just flew over the White House."

"That's not possible," Doug said. "I was on an instrument flight plan, following directions of the controller. If I was over the White House, that's where the controller put me."

"Just give me your name and address."

Doug complied, and proceeded to grab a taxi to Rockville, Maryland, where he completed his business as a reserve officer of the U.S. Public Health Service. The return flight to Westchester County Airport was uneventful.

After several weeks Doug received a letter from the FAA indicating they planned to suspend his license for thirty days unless he planned to object. If he filed an objection, his case would be decided by a magistrate of the National Transportation Safety Board.

Doug sure as hell objected. *I didn't fly over the White House, and they won't nail me for that.* He began to collect information.

He found that the guard at the White House had reported a red aircraft flying east to west over the White House at ten forty-seven. *I flew a blue aircraft from north to south, and at ten forty-seven my wheels were touching down at Washington National. This is confirmed by tower records.*

Doug called his Congressman, Lester Marino, and explained the situation.

"It appears that the FAA might be hassling you," Congressman Marino said. "I'll see what I can do."

The FAA sent one of their lawyers to meet with Doug at the Westchester Flight Service Station. Doug brought charts and all the information to show to the lawyer that he could not have flown over the White House. This lawyer didn't know a propeller from an aileron. After an hour and a half, the lawyer said, "I think we have a case, and I'm going to recommend that we move against you." A month later, Doug received another letter from the FAA offering to drop the charge against him if he would pay a fine of one hundred dollars. Doug sneered at the letter. *No way. I didn't do it, and I'm not going to pay.*

He received a phone call from Congressman Marino who told him, "The best I could do for you was to get your NTSB hearing moved to New York so you wouldn't have to go down to Washington."

"Thanks a lot," Doug said adding, "for nothing," after the call was terminated. *I guess I have to get a lawyer. One who specializes in Aviation Law.* Doug found one, and on a Sunday morning, he met with the lawyer in his office. Doug brought all the charts and evidence he had collected, and after he had presented his evidence to the lawyer, he was stunned when the lawyer told him, "Pay the fine."

"What?" Doug exploded.

"Look," the lawyer explained, "First of all, we would have to subpoena the tower controller and his records here to New York. You would have to pay his transportation and an overnight at a hotel. Secondly, you have to pay me for court time. Finally, I cannot guarantee the judge, after listening to our case, won't say, 'I'm going to find against you.' My advice is to pay the fine without admitting guilt. I'll write the letter for you."

Doug realized that was best, and in due course, sent a check for one hundred dollars to the FAA with the lawyer's letter.

And that seemed to be the end of it. Or so Doug thought. Perhaps six months later, Charlie had reason to call Congressman Marino on a matter relating to regulations dealing with swimming pools. Charlie was connected to the Congressman's secretary who responded, "Houser? Did you say your name was Houser? Aren't you the guy who flew over the White House?"

TAKING A CHANCE

On a fine Saturday morning in May, Kate awoke in high spirits. She anticipated spending the Memorial Day weekend with Matt, camping on the Delaware River. Matt told her he had a tent, a gas lantern, and a Prius stove, with some cooking implements. He said he knew of a good campground on the river near the Delaware Water Gap, where the river cuts through a large ridge of the Appalachian Mountains.

She dressed, pulling on jeans cut short to mid-thigh and a pink t-shirt. Breakfast was a bagel and a cup of coffee.

Kate met Matt two years ago at a conference in Reading. Matt O'Neil worked at a company in Allentown similar to Kate's, doing much the same thing. He was about her age and had a likable personality. At the conference, Kate and Matt often found themselves seated at the same table for discussions. They lunched together and discussed technical aspects of the meeting. Kate liked his open manner and his willingness to listen to what she had to say.

"Would you like to join me for dinner?" Matt asked, and Kate readily agreed. Matt was tall, good looking, and an outdoorsy type. Kate found they had common tastes in music, life style, and political persuasion. They dined together that evening and the following two nights. When the conference ended, they promised to keep in touch and to correspond by email, sharing technical information intermixed with their opinions on current events.

Kate met Matt at the convention the following year, and after a joyous reunion, they decided to share a hotel room. Kate threw her sleeping bag and her laptop in her 2016 Toyota, topped off the gas tank, and started on the Interstate for Pennsylvania crossing the Beacon Newburgh Bridge over the broad Hudson. Kate relaxed, listening to Stan Getz laying down cool jazz. She and

Matt were to meet for lunch at the diner in Milford, Pennsylvania. Kate liked Matt a lot, maybe she loved him. She hoped the intimacy of the tent might induce Matt to express any tender feelings he had for her.

Kate Morrison was one of the brightest students in her class at UCONN, graduating *Summa Cum Laude* with a degree in Computer Science and a minor in Psychology. For the past four years, she worked for a company in Hartford specializing in Artificial Intelligence.

Although the forecast predicted good weather for the weekend, it abruptly became dark when Kate turned onto the local road for Milford. The darkness progressed rapidly, and in a minute or two in was black as night, forcing Kate to turn on her headlights, and pull over to the shoulder of the road. She turned off the engine when there was a bright flash of lightening, followed by a tremendous thundercloud. Kate was frightened. She expected rain, but there was none.

After about ten minutes it began to lighten, and soon, Kate could see ahead. She saw that she had driven completely off the road, and began to back the car up onto the road. Suddenly, the car hit something. She figured she had struck another parked vehicle, and got out to investigate. To her surprise, she could not see anything there. She walked over to search the area. Maybe she had hit a large rock or a log, but she couldn't see anything. As she walked a few feet behind her car, she ran into something. It was like a wall, but it was invisible. When Kate used her hand to investigate, an electric shock ran up her arm. Cautiously, she explored the wall. It was higher than she could reach and appeared to cover the entire road. She could see through this wall, but things seemed blurry behind it.

Kate got back into her car and continued towards Milford. She had driven this route several times before, but now things looked different. The road now was barely paved, and she could not see the motel that used to be there. As she drove around a curve, she saw two men walking together. When they saw her car, they stopped and starred, gesturing wildly. Kate pulled over to them, stopped, and lowered her window.

"Could you tell me where the Milford Dinner is located," she asked." The men starred at her. They were looking at her car. One of the men walked slowly around her car while the other man starred at her with an expression of disbelief.

"Sir," Kate said. "When you have finished inspecting my car, could you direct me to the Milford Diner?" The man took off his hat. "I'm sorry Miss, but there ain't no Milford Diner here. I've lived here for forty-eight years. I wish we had a diner. It would be nice to eat out once in awhile. Can I ask where you got that car?"

"Japan," Kate said. She wanted to move on, but had to blow her horn to get the other man to move away from the front of the car. He jumped back, startled. Kate drove to the village she knew as Milford, but there was only a cluster of houses and an occasional store. Just ahead, there were three men engaged in a conversation, and Kate stopped her car and called to one of them. "Where is Milford," she asked, "What happened to it?" The man walked over to her car. "This here is Milford. Can I help you?" He asked.

"Is this a movie set or something?" Kate asked. She became confused. The man starred at her. "I don't know what you're talking about," he said. Kate noticed a sign reading, "Groceries and Tea." She parked in front and entered the store. There was a small counter with a man and a woman behind it. The man wore an apron, starred at Kate, and for a moment, they stood in silence. The woman asked Kate, "Would you like a cup of tea, Dear?" "Yes, please," Kate said, and sat down at the one small table. *This must be a country store,* she thought, *everything is so old fashioned.* Kate noticed a newspaper lying on the table. The headline read, "Roosevelt Rides in an Aeroplane." Kate began to read. "Former President Theodore Roosevelt rode in an aeroplane last week, the first President ever to do..." Kate looked at the date of the newspaper. May 12, 1910. The woman brought Kate a small pot of tea with containers of sugar and cream.

"Do you have any lemon?" Kate asked. The women shook her head. "We don't have lemons. That's a unusual outfit you're wearing," she said.

"Is this newspaper a souvenir?" Kate asked her.

"No, Dear, it's a real paper. They were just delivered a few days ago. Did you want to buy a copy?"

"Can I ask you, what is today's date?" Kate asked. The woman smiled. "Today is May fifteenth."

"What year?" Kate persisted.

"Nineteen-ten of course."

I've got to get out of here, Kate thought. She put a dollar bill on the table and left.

"Don't you want your change?" the woman called after her.

Kate got back into her car and began to drive. She turned on the radio, but all she could hear was static. *I guess I'm not going to find Matt here. I'll try to get to Allentown. At least that's a city. Maybe I can learn something there.*

It took Kate many hours to reach Allentown. There were no paved roads, and few signs, but she finally pulled into the city in the late afternoon. Like Milford, Allentown had changed. She was hungry, thirsty, and frightened. This was like a bad dream. *I don't think I'm going to find Matt here, but I need some essentials like food, clothing, and shelter.* Kate drove through what looked like a residential neighborhood, until she saw a sign, "Rooms for Rent." The place looked respectable. Kate stopped, parked in front, and entered. The place seemed clean. An older woman appeared. She starred at Kate's attire with a stern expression, then asked, "Can I help you?"

"I'd like to rent a room," Kate said.

"For how long?" The woman asked.

"I'm not sure," Kate said.

"I rent by the week, or by the month," the woman told her.

"I'll start by the week," Kate said, "how much?"

"Five dollars," the woman said. "I can provide dinner meals for seventy-five cents a day."

"May I see the room?"

The woman led her up two flights of stairs and down the hallway, stopping before a door. She took a key from her pocket and opened it. The room had a bed, a night table, and a dressing table. There was a pitcher and a basin on the dressing table. The bed was well made up and looked clean. Peering out the window, Kate could see the street. A small crowd had gathered around her car.

"I'll take it," Kate said.

The woman continued to look at Kate. "I don't permit men guests in the rooms at anytime," she said.

"That's fine," Kate said, "can you tell me where I can buy some clothing? Nothing fancy, just ordinary, plain clothes."

The woman's expression softened somewhat. "Marcy's is a good place for clothes. They're reasonable and a few blocks away. My name is Mrs. Miller," the woman said, "Sophie Miller. I hope you like it here."

"I'm Kate. Kate Morrison."

Kate was able to find Marcy's clothing store. Inside there were racks of dresses and blouses. Kate bought some underwear, several pairs of cotton stockings, and a few cotton blouses. She selected several cotton dresses and two skirts. She was amazed at how far her money went. She tried on the dresses and skirts. All were ankle length. Inquiring about shoes, she was directed to a shoe store on the next block, where she bought a pair of sensible shoes. Kate found a garage and drove in.

"I want to speak to the owner," she told the young man who came to help her.

"Yes, ma'am," he said, and the owner appeared. Like others, he starred at her Toyota in wonder.

"Where did you get this car?" he asked, his gaze fluctuated between her car and her outfit.

"It came from Japan," Kate said.

"How can I help you?" the owner asked.

"I want to store it here, so that no one else can see it," Kate said. "Do you have a place where you can hide it?"

The owner was thoughtful for a moment. "Yes Ma'am, I do. How long do you plan to keep it here?" he asked.

"Right now I don't know, but probably for a long time. How much will the storage cost?"

"How does a dollar a week sound?" he asked.

"It sounds ridiculous," Kate said. "I'll pay you fifty cents a week, not a penny more."

"It's a deal," the owner said.

"I want you to buy a big tarp. Big enough to cover the car. I'll pay for the tarp, and you can keep it when I'm gone."

"I can do that," the owner said.

"Fine. I'll bring the car by tomorrow." Kate drove back to the rooming house with her purchases and arranged to have dinner with Mrs. Miller. The meal was a simple stew with potatoes. There was bread and butter on the table, and a pitcher of water.

Afterwards, Kate retired to her room. She needed to think. *I've got to find out about this place—this time. Who could I ask?*

Also, my money won't last forever, even though it goes a long way here. Then she thought about Matt, and tears filled her eyes. *I guess I'll never find him here. I'll probably never see him again.* Kate fell asleep thinking of him, her job, her friends, and family.

The next morning when Kate woke, she hoped the whole thing had been a bad dream, until she opened her eyes. Kate found a bathroom down the hall and was able to shower and brush her teeth with the few toiletries she had brought. There were clean towels in her room. She dressed in one of her new dresses, pulled on cotton stockings, and began to think of breakfast. She yearned for a cup of coffee. She wrapped her shorts and t-shirt up, planning to store them in her car. Out of curiosity, she tried her laptop. The battery was still charged, but there was no Internet. She might as well store the laptop in the car. Kate returned the car to the garage and drove it to the place indicated by the owner. She left her laptop and sleeping bag in the car, and locked it, keeping the keys and walking around the city. For the next week, Kate familiarized herself with the neighborhood around her boarding house. Her mind was filled with questions. *Is there a way to get out of this place, this time? Maybe if I drove back to Milford that invisible wall might be gone, and I could just drive back to my time? May I'll try that later.* Kate knew the nearest large city was Philadelphia. *There must be a University there. Sure, UPenn. Maybe one of the professors might know about this time thing?*

Kate found that her boarding house had a telephone. Where there's a phone, there must be a phone book. *Maybe I could find a Philadelphia phone book somewhere.* After some thought, Kate decided to try City Hall. She found the phone had no dial. When she lifted the receiver a voice asked, "Number please?" She looked up the number for City Hall. It was BRYANT 709. She picked up the phone and asked for that number and was connected. "Does anyone there have a copy of the Philadelphia phone book?" she asked. She had reached the mayor's office. "I'm sure we have one," a voice said.

"Can I come over and look in it?" Kate asked. "I don't see why not," the secretary answered.

Kate walked over to City Hall the next day, and eventually was able to find a Philadelphia phone book. She looked for the University of Pennsylvania and found a number. She found a pencil and copied the number. There were no ballpoints in sight. She thanked the secretary, walked back to her boarding house, and placed a call to the University of Pennsylvania.

"Which department do you want?"

She asked for the Department of Physics and eventually was connected to a professor. Kate told him of her experience. "I know it's hard to believe," she said, "but here I am."

"It is hard to believe," the professor said, "and even if it were true, I would have no idea how to help you. I'm sorry," he said and disconnected.

So much for that, Kate thought. *Well, unless I get some kind of a break, I guess I'm here to stay. I'm going to have to find a job.*

Kate soon found that the clerks in every store she visited were men. The only place she could think of where she knew women were employed were as teachers. She contacted the Allentown Board of Education and applied for a job. At first, her application was rejected. She had no academic record that she could show, that she had graduated from a Normal School. But then, there was a vacancy. A teacher for a summer school class in math was needed, and they agreed to give Kate a chance. She would be teaching algebra. The students were all boys about twelve years old, and Kate did just fine. The students loved her, and thought she was terrific. Their performance on a final exam so impressed the Board of Education that they agreed to let Kate continue teaching through the regular school year as well. Now

Kate had a salary. It was laughable by her standards...four hundred and ten dollars a year, but it was better than nothing.

One weekend, Kate decided to try driving back to her time. She drove her Toyota back to Milford, slowly approaching the place where the invisible wall had been. After walking over and trying to feel the wall, she gingerly drove past it. She continued to drive, but her heart sank. The road was not well paved, and eventually she reached Newburgh and the river. There was no bridge. She drove towards the river. *Perhaps there's a ferry.* As she drew closer, the road grew steeper and muddier, and Kate moved faster towards the river than she wanted. She saw the river coming up fast, and she put on the breaks, but that didn't stop the car, it continued to slip in the mud towards the river. In a panic, Kate jumped out. She watched as her car slid on the mud, moving faster until at the end of the road, it slid into the river, sinking under the water.

Kate was stunned. "I just lost my laptop and my sleeping bag," she said. Then, ever the optimist, she thought, *well I won't have to pay storage anymore.* She cried and laughed, and then started to hike back. It took Kate two days and nights to reach Milford, where she found a man with a horse and carriage to drive her back to Allentown. Back at her rooming house, she took a hot bath and slept for a whole day. When she woke again, she realized that for better or worse, she was here to stay. She had a roof over her head and a salary.

The years passed. Kate became more comfortable. She now rented her room by the month, and took most of her meals with Mrs. Miller. Ten years passed. Kate had little opportunities to meet other people. At school, she met other teachers, women, most of whom were older than Kate. She took pleasure with each class of young boys that she spent a term with, teaching them algebra. Most were of average intelligence, a few were bright, but they all were serious about learning and studied hard.

One September, Kate met her new class. She sat at her desk and called the role. Jones, Martin, O'Neil. The boy said, "here."

"What is your first name?" she asked.

"Matthew, Ma'am."

Her heart jumped. She studied him. Yes, she could see a similarity. After the class was over, she asked Matthew to remain in the room.

"I have a few questions I'd like to ask you Matthew, if you don't mind."

"No Ma'am, I don't mind."

"First of all, how old are you?"

"I'm twelve."

"Could you tell me something about your family? Do you have any brothers or sisters?"

"Yes Ma'am, I have an older brother, Jon, and a younger sister, Elizabeth."

"Thank you, Matthew, you can go."

Now she was sure. Everything the boy told her corresponded with what she knew about Matt. This was her Matt. *Twelve years old, and I'm thirty-four. In ten years, he will be twenty-two, and I will be forty-four. Well,* she thought, *if I kept myself in good shape, exercise, watch my diet, just maybe... it's a possibility. I'll chance it.*

SMALL MIRACLE IN SAN MIGUEL

On a warm evening in January, Esperanza Lopez and her daughter Conchita walked along the cobblestone street past the church. They waved to Father Donovan who smiled as the bride and groom left the church. Worshippers streamed out of the church and strolled toward the plaza to watch the Sunday night entertainment. Most of them were short, their olive skin and straight black hair attesting to their Mayan ancestry.

Father Donovan retired to the rectory. He sat on the small porch idly watching the swallows flying to their nests under the eaves. He recalled the island had been named for them, Cozumel, Mayan for "Place of the Swallows". The priest had been with this small church for six years since his last post in County Meath. He came to love the island and its people, hardworking, friendly Mexicans with an admixture of Mayan blood.

Esperanza and Conchita joined the other natives who had come to enjoy the spectacle. The two found a vacant place on one of the benches lining the dance floor. Esperanza began to chat with a neighbor.

In ancient days, Mayan maidens crossed twelve miles of water in dugout canoes from the Yucatan mainland to visit the island and worship Ixtel, the goddess of fertility. Then, the Spanish Conquistadors came bringing Christianity and smallpox. Smallpox decimated the Mayan civilization leaving the survivors to accept Christianity. The Virgin Mary replaced Ixtel, Jesus took the place of Kukulkan, and the saints, thinly disguised, replaced Chac Mool and the other gods. Mayans eventually settled on the island. In time, newcomers from Mexico City, who became owners of taxis, dive shops and restaurants, joined them. Many of the Mayans, like Esperanza, found jobs in the hotels now bordering the many beaches along the western shore of the island.

Conchita, who was twelve, wore a pale green dress with purple and black polka dots and shiny black shoes. This evening she wore a pair of her mother's earrings, having convinced her mother to lend the small gold hoops.

"Please, please Momma, just this once. I'll be careful."

Esperanza finally consented. "You'd better not lose them. Your Papa would kill me."

Esperanza continued to chat with her neighbor, partly in Mayan, and Conchita was becoming bored.

"Momma," she asked, "may I have an ice cream?" Esperanza smiled and gave the girl a coin.

"Here, Chita, make sure you get change." The girl dashed off.

The plaza was lined on three sides by streets with shops and restaurants, the fourth side open to the Malecon, a long road that wound along the sea past the many hotels and beaches. In the center of the plaza there was a large stone dance floor with a wooden bandstand. Taxis began to stop disgorging visitors who walked to the plaza anxious to view the festivities.

As the twilight deepened, the bell in the clock tower at the rear of the plaza struck six and activity became livelier. Young children ventured onto the dance floor to chase each other while musicians took their places on the bandstand. The churro man set up his small stand and soon the scent of the sweet frying dough filled the air. A man, wearing a huge sombrero garishly decorated with silver thread, walked around the plaza offering his floating balloons to the crowd without success. The local women sat together on benches talking animatedly while the visitors stood around watching them, waiting for the music to start.

It was now quite dark and floodlights lit the plaza. The bandleader, using a microphone, invited everyone to dance. The music was loud with a Latin beat. The visitors began to dance while the locals watched.

Conchita returned to join her mother who continued to talk with her neighbor. As the girl sat licking her cone, a large grasshopper flew over to land on her lap. She picked up the insect and released it into the shrubbery.

"Shoo, grasshopper. Go back to where you belong." Conchita absently touched her right ear only to discover to her horror the precious earring was missing. She panicked. *It must have dropped off*! She thought. *Momma will kill me when she finds out I lost it. I have to find it!* Conchita got up and began to walk along the edge of the plaza searching the ground retracing her steps to the ice cream stand.

"Wait," Esperanza called. "*Tush bekan*?" In asking Conchita where she was going, Esperanza forgot that the girl, like the rest of her generation, did not speak the Mayan tongue.

As Conchita searched, she tried to imagine what she would say to her mother. She knew she would never be able to find it, but continued to look. Her desperation deepened as she neared the ice cream stand. Something gleamed on the ground. Yes! There it is—the small gold hoop. Conchita ran over to pick it up, almost colliding with a boy eating an ice cream cone. The boy, about her age, was white and one of the visitors. He ignored her, picked up the earring, examined it and put it into his pocket. Conchita stared at him, uncomprehending, not knowing what to do. She took a few steps toward him and stopped. What can I do? She thought. I can't speak his language.

The boy took no notice of her and continued to walk around the plaza. Conchita followed him until he found his parents. She watched as he took the earring from his pocket and showed it to them. The boy said something to them she did not understand, his parents nodded, and the boy put the earring back into his pocket. Conchita followed them as they strolled back to the Malecon and watched in dismay as they hailed a taxi and drove off.

Conchita was in no hurry to rejoin her mother and tell her about the lost earring. Maybe she won't notice that the earring is missing, she thought. She dawdled along the street on the opposite side of the plaza from where her mother sat, looking into the shops, paying no attention to the music. When Conchita heard the bandleader announce the last dance, she hurried back to Esperanza.

"Where have you been?" her mother asked as they walked home. "I called after you and—oh, you've lost an earring!"

"No," the girl said. "I lent it to a friend."

"How could you do such a thing? Your father gave me those earrings. You begged to wear them, and then you go and lend one to someone. Is that all you think of me?"

The girl began to cry as her mother continued to upbraid her. Finally Conchita told her mother.

"I didn't lend it. I lost it. It must have dropped off my ear. I looked all over for it. I'm sorry, Momma."

"Why did you lie?"

"I don't know," the girl sobbed. She told her mother how the boy, one of the visitors, found it.

"Then we'll never see it again," Esperanza said.

Monday morning, Conchita went to the church and entered the confessional.

"Bless me, Father, for I have sinned." Father Donovan recognized Conchita. "I told a lie to my mother."

"Why did you lie?" the Priest asked.

Conchita explained about the earring.

"Lying is not good, my child, but then you told the truth. However, you showed disrespect to your mother. For your penance, say two Hail Mary's and two Our Father's."

The girl left the confessional to kneel and pray. These people take religion seriously, the Priest thought. He wondered if Conchita prayed to the Blessed Virgin or to Ixtel. The old religion dies slowly, the Priest thought, and Jesus Christ still competes with Chac Mool and Kukulkan.

"Momma," Conchita said later. "I confessed to Father Donovan and told him all about the earring. I'm so sorry."

"Well," Esperanza told her, "what's done is done. The earring is gone forever."

On the same morning, Esperanza went to work. Employed as a maid by one of the large hotels, she cleaned room after room, all the while considering how she would tell Francisco about the earring. She knew her husband would be upset to say the least.

By eight o'clock, she cleaned one of the rooms after observing the occupants, a man, woman and a boy, leave. Esperanza saw the remnants of their breakfast on the small balcony. Something on the table caught her attention. She looked more closely and could not believe her eyes. There it was—the simple gold hoop. It was her earring! A voice in her head said, take it, it's yours. You got it back. But a lower voice said, you cannot. It's stealing. You could lose your job. Esperanza was in torment. Even though the earring belonged to her, she could not take it. Sick at heart, she left the treasured earring it in its place, and continued her daily routine.

At five o'clock her work was finished. She rode the bus for the short ride into town and walked to the church. Inside Father Donovan was finishing up following the afternoon devotions. Esperanza walked over to him and clutched his sleeve.

"Father, I must tell you. You won't believe it. I found my earring." She proceeded to relate where she found the earring. "But, I couldn't take it."

Father Donovan consoled her. "You did the right thing, Esperanza. God must be testing you." Esperanza turned and started home.

Father Donovan went to the rectory, poured himself a glass of lemonade and sat on the porch. How strange, he thought. Was it sheer coincidence the woman saw her earring? He was impressed by her forbearance. As he mused, he noticed what appeared to be a small mound of dried mud on the porch floor. His housekeeper, one of the local women, was meticulous in keeping the rectory clean. She must have missed it. Curious, the Priest went over to inspect it. It was a nest. It must have fallen from under the eaves. As he bent to pick it up, something small and shiny fell from the nest. He looked closer. "Holy Mary, Mother of God!" he exclaimed. It was the small gold hoop that Esperanza had just described. How—? One of the swallows caught the Priest's attention. The bird fluttered under the eaves making loud sounds. Then he understood. Somehow the bird had picked up the earring from the hotel balcony and brought it here to its nest. Father Donovan was stunned. This was supernatural. He retrieved the earring and hurried to catch up with Esperanza. Her eyes grew wide with amazement as he handed her the earring.

"It's beautiful, Father," she said, handing the earring back to him.

"Take it, Esperanza. It's yours."

Tears filled her eyes. "No, Father. It's not mine. It's beautiful but it's different. Look, see." She removed an earring from her ear and showed it to the Priest. It was similar but indeed different.

"I want you to have it, Esperanza. God wants you to have it. He sent it to you."

The woman took the earring hesitantly. "How? How did God send it?"

What explanation can I offer? He pondered. The words from the old William Cowper hymn. "God works in mysterious ways, His wonders to perform," the Priest said, and walked back to the church.

The town was quiet, the Mexicans were in their homes, and the visitors had departed. Dusk fell on the empty plaza as the bell in the clock tower chimed six. It seemed to the priest a spirit of peace and rectitude permeated the air. Father Donovan sighed. Perhaps this was indeed a miracle.

CONNECTION

On a bright morning, a man could be seen driving west along I-287. He crossed the Tappan Zee Bridge, which spans the broad Hudson and continued to Route 303 where he turned south. After the small village of Blauvelt, he left the highway, drove a few blocks and pulled up in front of his destination. It was April 7th and Spring was evidenced by the profusion of yellow forsythia and daffodils.

Alex Schaefer made the trip on this date for many years. He parked in front of the cemetery. The burial ground was a small one, not much larger than a square city block, backed up by a patch of woods. It was well maintained, set unobtrusively in a quiet neighborhood near a high school. The cemetery was enclosed by an iron fence supported at intervals by tall stone pillars and bisected by a low railing separating the occupants by faith—Christians on their acre, Jews on theirs.

Alex entered the open gate carrying a small bunch of daffodils and walked toward the rear of the cemetery where his father's grave lay. There were no other visitors and only the chirping of birds disturbed the quiet. As he approached his father's resting place, rehearsing the brief family summary he always delivered, he saw something black on his father's grave. A blackbird or a crow he guessed, but whatever it was remained stationary as he drew nearer. The object rested on the small footstone that read "George Schaefer, 1899-1975, A Man for All Seasons". It was a telephone! The telephone was an old-fashioned one with a shiny black handset resting on a low base with a rotary dial. He was astonished to see a cord ran from the phone and plunged into the grave.

Some prankster Alex presumed—a macabre joke. He looked around, half expecting to see a few high school kids in the woods or hear derisive laughter. On an impulse, he lifted the handset to his ear and was stunned to hear a dial tone. He dropped the handset into the cradle and stood staring at the instrument. Alex felt stupid.

Many years earlier, while hunting geese on Maryland's Eastern Shore, Alex came upon what appeared to be a flock of geese feeding in a field. He crawled on his belly for twenty minutes hoping to get within range before they flew off, but when he stood up to shoot, there was no movement. He had been stalking a bunch of decoys. Chagrined by his faux pas, Alex was certain unseen eyes were laughing at him. He felt ridiculous then as now.

Alex tried to pull the cord out of the grave expecting to find a cable to the woods, but the cord resisted. He picked up the handset again. The dial tone was still there. He remembered an old phone number the family had when he was young—DEfender 3-7367. On a whim, he dialed the number. It rang.

"Hello?" It was his father's voice.

Alex's heart leaped in his chest. He could never forget the musical, professorial quality with its clear enunciation and friendly timbre. His father was his best friend, supporting him during the difficult days of his childhood. He died taking Alex's two sons to the circus. More than anything else, Alex wanted to speak to him. He could hear a radio in the background, Ethel Merman singing, "You're the Tops".

"Who's calling?" His father asked.

"Dad, it's Alex, your son, Alex. I wanted to wish you a Happy Birthday."

"You must have the wrong number. My son is here in his room. Sorry, I can't help you."

"Wait! Don't hang up." There was a click. Alex was talking to a dial tone. He dialed the number again, getting a busy signal. After a minute, he tried again, still busy. Alex kept dialing over and over to no avail.

Finally, he dialed “O” and a voice said “Operator”.

“Operator, I’m trying to reach a number, and it’s always busy.”

“What is the number? I’ll try it for you,” she said. He gave her the number.

“I’m sorry, sir. That number is no longer in service.”

“But I just—.” Dial tone.

Alex felt frustrated. He dialed “O” again and when the operator came on, he said, “I’d like to speak with your supervisor.”

“One moment, sir.” After a minute, another voice came on.

“A short time ago I was connected to a number. Then I got busy signals and now the operator tells me the number is no longer in service.”

“What was that number?”

“DEfender 3-7367,” Alex told her.

After a pause, she said, “Sir, the DEfender exchange hasn’t been used for 40 years.”

“But I just spoke . . . ” Alex expostulated.

“I’m sorry, sir. There’s nothing I can do.” Dial tone.

Incredible as it seemed, he had actually spoken a few words to his long dead father. Now, he wanted to continue. Here was a chance for him to talk to his father again, and it was being taken away from him. Alex became irritated. Then he remembered another phone number his father had used, perhaps ten or more years after the first number. HAvemeyer 3-6624. His hand trembled as he dialed it. It was ringing. Once again he heard his father’s voice. This time his father spoke somewhat slower. He sounded older.

"Hi, Dad," he said. "It's Alex. Happy Birthday."

"Thanks, Alex. Where are you?"

Alex did not know what to say. He could not tell his father he was at his grave. He ignored the question.

"I'm fine, Dad. How are you?"

Someone in the room spoke to his father.

"Just a minute, Alex," he said, but after a moment the connection was broken by the dial tone. Alex frantically redialed, but got a busy signal. He dialed the operator again and was advised, "I'm sorry, sir. That number is no longer in service."

That was it. He could not think of any other old phone numbers. Reluctantly he drove home in a state of depression. Alex spent the evening searching old documents trying vainly to find other phone numbers. He called his brother who was able to provide one.

"Why do you need those?" His brother asked.

"Just doing some research," Alex said.

Alex tried calling the number his brother had given him as well as the other two old numbers, but nothing worked. Somehow he felt it had to be the phone in the cemetery.

Alex spent a troubled night filled with dreams like old family photographs. After a quick breakfast, he drove back across the river clutching the scrap of paper with the number his brother had given him. This time he knew he would succeed. He really wanted to speak with his father again, if only to tell him all was well. He pushed the speed limit.

The day was overcast when he reached the cemetery. He walked to the grave, but something was different. The phone was gone. He could not believe it. He knew the phone had been there yesterday. Or had it? Was yesterday's experience a figment of his imagination? Was the telephone episode a fantasy?

Alex got down on his hands and knees to examine the turf over the grave. There it was. Just behind the footstone he saw it, a hole about an inch in diameter where the cord from the phone had entered the soil. It was unmistakable. He had not imagined it.

Alex grew angry. It wasn't fair. He was certain the number his brother had given him would have connected. He got up and stood by the grave, considering what to do. A light rain began to fall.

"I'm sorry, Dad," he said aloud. "I tried." He turned and walked back to the car.

Driving home, Alex's thoughts vacillated like the windshield wipers. Who or what had put the phone there? And why? Was it some kind of a test? Maybe a reward, but for what? Why me? These questions tortured Alex to the extent he left the highway, pulled off to a quiet adjoining street and parked. The only thing he knew for certain was after all these years he had been permitted to hear his father's voice again. His mind sought answers. He had to go back.

At the cemetery he walked to the gravesite and stood staring at the footstone. The daffodils still lay there, but the rain had turned the soil into mud, and the hole where the cord had been was becoming obscured. Yet Alex was sure the experience had been real. He even recalled the smell of the handset when he had clutched it to his face. Alex imagined in the infinite number of human experiences, there must be some, beyond reason or understanding, defying explanation.

But then a thought occurred to him. If this had happened once, it could happen again. He would not tell anyone about it, but when he returned each year on his father's birthday, there was always the possibility the phone would be there. Although it was only a taste, it was enough.

"Thanks," he murmured to no one in particular.

Crossing the bridge, the rain stopped and the sky brightened. He turned off the windshield wipers.

Alex walked in his front door to be greeted by his wife.

"What happened? You're soaking wet," she exclaimed.

Alex kissed her and smiled. "Something quite wonderful," he said.

THE THIRTY-SIXTH MAN

There is an ancient legend in Jewish, Islamic and Persian folklore concerning the thirty-six just men. These men or women are righteous, wise, and compassionate. Tradition holds that the existence of the world rests on these thirty-six. When one of them dies, another replaces him. Unaware they are members of a special group, they live throughout the world doing good.

The President was working alone at his desk in the Oval Office when he became aware of another presence. He looked up and was startled to see a man standing before his desk. The man appeared to be in his 70's, possibly 80's. He was mostly bald, with a ring of gray hair around the crown of his head, dressed in clean blue jeans and a long sleeved western shirt open at the neck. The man did not appear to be armed or represent an immediate threat.

The President's first impulse was to press a button, which would bring Secret Service agents rushing into the office, but he did not do so. "How—how did you get in here?" the President started to ask but changed his mind. "Who are you?"

The old man smiled. "My name is Daniel," he said.

"Daniel what?" the President asked.

"Just Daniel," the old man said. The President became somewhat more relaxed. "I thought you might need some help," the old man said.

"Some help?" the President chuckled. "You know, Daniel, I have a Cabinet and a whole flock of advisors of every kind. What kind of help could you possibly give me?"

"I don't know," said the old man, "somehow I just thought you might need some help."

"Well," the President mused, "there is one controversial problem that has been bothering me."

"The oil leak in the Gulf," Daniel said.

"Right," the President said. "It's troublesome. The Republicans . . . are you a Republican?" he asked.

"No, I'm not registered with either party," Daniel said.

"Good, you're an Independent," the President said. "We Americans want to get out from under the pressures the Arabs hold us to with respect to oil. You're not an Arab are you?"

"No, Mister President, I'm not."

"Good," the President said. "You see the Democrats are concerned about the environment . . ."

"Yes, I know," the old man said. "It's troubling because both sides have valid points."

The President nodded in agreement.

"But, you could handle it by a sort of compromise."

"What sort of compromise?" asked the President.

"Well, Mister President, suppose you got the Congress to pass strict legislation regulating the oil companies and making them responsible for any damages they might do to the environment. At the same time you could somehow use the oil already in the Gulf."

"That's a good idea," the President said. He got up from his desk and faced the large window. "Look out there," he said, "the people depend on me to make the right decisions. It's hard to please them all." He turned to face Daniel, but the old man was gone. I've been working too hard—I've been fantasizing. But later at a meeting of the Cabinet, he thought of the idea. He thought it was his own and mentioned it.

***

The evening TV anchor described the case of little Michael Alvarez, a smiling four year old with dark eyes and curly hair. "Michael has a fatal disease," he announced, "and his doctors are desperately trying to find someone whose bone marrow cells match Michael's. His parents are asking for volunteers."

At the hospital the next day the old man appeared in the line of volunteers. There were only a few. When it became his turn the nurse asked his name. "Daniel," he said.

"Daniel what?"

"Just Daniel."

"Oh, you must have a last name," the nurse said.

Michael's parents were standing by. "Please just test him," they said. "His last name could be Daniels."

"Okay," the nurse said and obtained a specimen from Daniel. In a short time the child's parents and the doctors were elated to learn Daniel's cells matched Michael's.

Mrs. Alvarez became excited. "Are you really willing to donate some cells to our son?" she asked.

"Yes," the old man said.

"When can you do it?" the nurse said. "It has to be pretty soon."

"Why not right now?" Daniel said.

"We can do that," the nurse said.

Within an hour, the old man lay on a table in an adjoining room. After sterilizing the skin over his hip, the doctors obtained some of his bone marrow cells. The procedure was somewhat painful and when they were finished, Daniel walked with a slight limp.

Several weeks later the doctors announced the transfusion had been successful, and there was every hope Michael's disease had been cured. Michael's parents were excited and happy. Mrs. Alvarez decided she had to thank the old man. When she called the hospital, it appeared there was no record of the old man's telephone number, but he had given an address in Queens. Mrs. Alvarez bought a large bouquet of flowers, and Mr. Alvarez bought a bottle of whiskey. Together they traveled to the address in Queens. They knocked at the door. A black woman opened the door and looked at them curiously.

"We're here to see Daniel or Mister Daniels," Mrs. Alvarez announced.

"Ain't nobody here by that name," the woman said.

"Oh, but this is the address the hospital gave us."

"I been living here for nigh on 24 years," the woman said. "There's nobody here like that." Mrs. Alvarez looked disappointed. The black woman added, "I'm sorry, there ain't no Daniel here."

***

The old man sat on the bottom steps of a brownstone in Harlem warming himself in the late September sun. A boy about fifteen shuffled by carrying schoolbooks.

The old man smiled at him. "Hi," he said.

The boy stopped and looked at the old man. He was curious at the white face in this neighborhood.

"Hey," said the boy.

"What's your name?" the old man asked.

"James," the boy said. "What's yours?"

"Daniel," the old man said. "Why don't you come, and sit here awhile, and we'll talk?"

"Okay, I got nothing better to do," the boy said, and sat down next to the old man.

Daniel produced a Baby Ruth candy bar from his pocket, broke it in half, and shared it with the boy. James took it, and they both ate in silence.

"How's school coming along?" the old man asked.

"Not too good," the boy said, somewhat disconsolately.

"What's the problem?"

"It's math. I just don't understand it."

"Maybe I could help?" Daniel told him.

"You know math?" James asked.

"I know some".

The boy opened his book and showed the problem to Daniel. It was algebra. "See," James said, "it's these x's and y's, and stuff with the numbers. I just don't get it."

"It's easy," Daniel said. "They use 'x' to mean something you want to find out, a number. And when there are two things you want to find out, they have the second thing be 'y'."

"How about solving the problem?" the boy asked hopefully.

"Well," Daniel said, "math is like this. You know the plus sign?"

"Yeah," James said. "It means to add."

"Right, and the minus sign, it means to take away. And the 'x' means to multiply. And the minus sign with the two dots means to divide. You see," the old man said "everything in math has an opposite. Add, subtract, multiply, divide, and so on. It's like life, good and bad.

Together they worked through some of the simple problems, and in a short time the old man had helped the boy finish his homework.

"Say man, are you a white nig—?"

Daniel held up his hand. "That's not a good word to use, James. I'm white just like you're black."

"OK," the boy said. "Thanks."

"Sure thing," the old man said as the boy picked up his books and started home.

The next day Daniel was sitting on the steps again when James came by in the afternoon.

"Hi," Daniel said.

"Hey," James said and without being asked, he sat down on the step next to Daniel. "You got time for a little more math?" the boy asked. "The teacher has confused me again."

Daniel went through the problems with the boy.

"Oh, I get it. It's easy," James said.

Over the next few weeks, James passed Daniel every day, sometimes with just a wave and a smile, other times to sit for more help. The weeks stretched into months. If it rained or the weather was cold, Daniel invited James into the kitchen for a cup of hot chocolate.

One day, when James was in his senior year, Daniel asked him what he planned to do after graduation.

"I want to be a doctor," James said, "if I can get into college and medical school."

"You can do it," Daniel told him. "You're a bright young man, and you work hard."

A few months later, James received a letter from a university granting him admission. He was overjoyed, and after sharing this information with his parents, he rushed to the brownstone to tell the news to Daniel.

Although the weather was fine, Daniel was not on the steps where he usually sat. James ran up the steps and knocked at the door. No one answered, but James found the door was unlocked. He went into the kitchen. The apartment was deserted. There was no furniture, but on the kitchen table there was a small black doctor's bag. On it there was a note that read "For James".

***

The journey was a long one but Daniel knew he had to go. After many days he found himself in a strange place where the people dressed differently and spoke a new language. Daniel walked down a deserted road, which entered dense woods. He still walked with a slight limp. The road branched into three paths, and Daniel did not know which one to take. He was very tired and sat down on a rock at the side of the road. A man walked down the road and stopped in front of Daniel. He looked to be about 40.

"Can I help?" the man asked.

"Well, yes," Daniel said, "I don't know which path to take."

"The path on the left ends in a swamp," the man said, "and the path on the right leads to a desert. The middle path will take you where you want to go."

"Thanks," Daniel said. "May I ask your name?"

The man smiled. "Daniel," the man said, "just Daniel."

ACKNOWLEDGEMENTS

Samantha Lovetere prepared the manuscript and helped in researching factual information. My daughter, Diane Meyers, Casey Rafferty, and my brother Sidney Ellner read the first draft and contributed helpful comments. Finally, my wife Connie spent long hours editing and reviewing the manuscript. Art work by Tovero and Marks.

CPSIA information can be obtained
at www.ICGtesting.com
Printed in the USA
FFOW03n0905061217
43873024-42857FF

9 781634 926621